Beyond the Scent of Sugar

A Memoir by Billie Rivers

Montana Carr

Northshore Noir

Northshore Noir Press
Toronto, Canada
www.northshorenoir.com

ISBN Hardcover: 978-1-0688501-3-4
ISBN Paperback: 978-1-0688501-2-7
ISBN e-Book 978-1-0688501-4-1

Contents

Introduction

I met Martina Starova–Marti–in the spring of '49. I was in my bakery when a middle-aged man came scurrying in. It was pouring rain, so everyone was scurrying in. He headed right for a table in the back. There were only 5 tables–it's a bakery after all. He came in, sat down and then, maybe 10 seconds later, Marti came in.

Strike that.

Marti blasted in. The door slammed open, and she raced in, bringing the storm with her. I don't think she touched the floor, but just flew. The man stood up to flee. She made a flying tackle. Both ended up hitting my window and the cracking sound was louder than the thunder. Then onto the floor, grunting and screaming and cursing.

Marti was punching him, and he was punching Marti. I could see she had a gun–or at least a holster–and I wondered why she didn't just shoot him. By the time that thought was in my head and I'd reached for my phone to call the police, Marti was on her feet. She snatched a chair and swung, hitting him hard. The chair broke, of course–it was just cheap plasprint after all. He swung a table in return, then launched her into a display case. Shards of glass and blood went everywhere.

But it didn't stop her. I've since found out nothing stops her. She tackled him again, sending them both right through another of my windows, and out into the street. Only now did everyone else arrive. And by everyone else I mean uniformed police and detectives in cop cars with wailing sirens. It surprised me when they arrested him, not her. I mean, this normal guy comes in, followed by a wild woman who attacked him. Right?

Nothing is as it seems with Marti. It turned out he had murdered a couple and kidnapped their five-year-old daughter. The police had tracked him down and he had somehow slipped through their perimeter. He chose my bakery to hide in, and he failed.

She came back into the shop, bloodied and breathless, with Damien Kane, her partner. He was shouting at her for being an irresponsible asshole. She was laughing at him for being a fat fuck. Their words, not mine. By then, all of my customers had fled, and the rain was blowing in.

I will never forget that surge of electricity when she first looked me in the eye. She has a sexiness, a sexual magnetism, that is undeniable. This in spite of the fact she was bleeding from a cut over her eye and blood coated her lips. I find that bruised-and-bloodied look to be repulsive. But somehow, she made it work for her.

Marti offered me her business card–Martina Starova, Falls City Police, Homicide Division, Detective First Class. She said to call her and she would help me navigate the administrative systems to get reimbursed for the damage. Then she asked for a danish. All I could do was wordlessly point to the shattered display case and the glass-covered danishes.

She said she'd take a raspberry danish. She even said please, but I think that was so she could throw her killer smile at me. I told her I couldn't sell them, and she said she'd take it for free. I said they were covered in glass, and she asked if there was "one under the counter or something." Unbelievable.

Then Marti walked behind the display case, looked over the food, and picked a raspberry danish, and shook it off. She took a big bite and screamed, clutching her mouth. I ran over to her, grabbing her face to see what the damage was. Marti just laughed and said, "Psych! Just kidding." Joking like a damned 10-year-old.

Marti made a quick phone call before leaving. Within half an hour, a repair truck pulled up with some enormous pieces of plywood. They sealed my windows and said someone would be in touch about everything else. They said don't bother calling my insurance company.

I never called her, but I never had to. The next day, Falls City employees were swarming over my bakery. Glass replaced, floors cleaned and sterilized, new furniture, even nicer display cases installed. I got a $5,000 check to cover food and incidentals.

Marti made one hell of an impression on me. I followed the news for a couple of days. She was praised for her pursuit and arrest of that man.

She came by every once in a while for a danish until she stopped coming by. I didn't see her for four years, though I hadn't forgotten her.

I don't think anyone can forget Marti.

Chapter 1

It was raining. Of course. I hadn't heard from Marti for four years. Those were her four years in hell, which have nothing to do with me. Except the aftermath. It's like moving into a house after the flood waters have receded. You can't be sure how deep the damage goes, but you go in knowing it won't be perfect.

Marti had come by the bakery out of the blue. I almost fainted. I hadn't thought it possible, but she looked wilder and more erotic. Her black hair framed her face like a mane. Where once she had been a young lion, now she was a mature beast with battle scars and street wisdom. She had become a king of the jungle.

She left the police services and became a private investigator.

She had a hungry smile, and I wasn't sure if she wanted food or me. But she asked for a danish, and when I asked if she wanted raspberry, her eyes lit up. I told her to grab a seat and I'd bring it to her. Crazy as it sounds, her face softened. Like no one had done anything kind for her in a long time.

I don't think she actually likes raspberry danish, I think she just likes eating it. And I came up with this theory when I brought her the danish. Marti asked me to join her when I put the plate down. Ask is the wrong word. I was compelled in the nicest way possible. I sat down, and her eyes focused on mine, and I couldn't look away. Then she tore a piece from the danish and slipped it into her mouth. I watched her lick the glaze off her fingers. Never have I ever seen such pleasure in a public place. She dipped her finger into the raspberry and offered it to me. I couldn't stop my mouth from opening, from closing my lips around her, from sucking and licking. I could see she was getting aroused. I certainly was. And when I finally released her finger, she put it in her own mouth. I shivered. She ripped another piece off, stretching the pastry between her fingers before it came apart. I almost came apart. The overhead light dimmed, I swear.

She leaned over and brought the danish to my lips. I have eaten more bites of danish than I care to admit. Tasting is part of baking. But this wasn't just a bite of danish. This was a sticky, sweet, gooey nugget in my mouth. She watched me as I took it from her fingers, and she licked them clean.

"I'm going to kiss you." She was so confident. It wasn't a question, but a statement of fact. She very purposefully stood up and came around to my side of the table. My eyes never left her. I just looked up and felt my breath. She bent down and paused, looking into my eyes. Whatever she was searching for, she must have found. I felt a shock go through me, from her lips to my pussy, shooting straight down when she kissed me.

She smelled of cigarettes and booze, two things I don't like. Didn't like. Marti somehow made it seem earthy, musky. Like sex. No. Like lust. I heard the creak of her leather jacket as she reached for my chin. She was gentle as she raised my head a little more and kissed me again, harder. Suddenly I could smell the leather where I hadn't before. It mingled and mixed with her aroma, a personal perfume signature that now included raspberry danish and desire.

With each kiss, she pressed a little harder. And with each kiss, I got a bigger and bigger shock through my body. When her fingers moved and her thumb stroked my cheek, a lightning bolt shot through me and my pussy got wet. I remember thinking, is this what it's like to black out from pleasure? I moaned when she released me, and I leaned forward to offer myself to her again. But she sat down again. And she squeezed and pulled the danish again and I almost fainted when she ate it.

I was too light-headed to stand, so I remained there. Watching her lick and chew and feast. It felt like I was watching her eat me. She complimented me on my baking skills. I said it was nothing special. "It is to me," she said. As she put the last piece into her mouth, she asked me to meet her on Wednesday at 10pm at the Findlay on Jacob. I nodded, and she stood up. As I hoped, she kissed me one last time and walked out. I was grateful for the apron I was wearing because I was certain my nipples were hard and, quite possibly, my dress was wet.

Chapter 2

I didn't get nervous until the taxi pulled up to the Findlay. I got out, but I didn't see her. Not at first. Like any good predator, she hid from view until it was too late. I wasn't able to run for my life. She stepped out from behind a tree–how animalistic–and stood in the light that cut through the fog. My heart skipped when I saw her eyes. I could see a flicker of lust in hers. She wanted it and pulled me into her, kissing me hard. Her lips were hungry and her tongue flicked and probed. Tasted. "Wow." Even her leather jacket was perfect for her: dirty and scarred. Like battle armor.

I could feel all the right muscles contract. I think she felt them too, because she squeezed my hips right before she let me go. She told me I looked delicious and then, with her arm around my waist, guided me to the restaurant door. She opened the door for me. Something I figured out later she only did if she liked you.

The restaurant was busy, but had a homey warmth to it. Words were a low hum. Light moved like candle light.

Like everything was whispering. She whispered too, or so it seemed at first. She leaned down and I could feel her hot breath on my cheek, her lips on my ear. When I asked her to repeat that, she smiled, leaned over and nibbled on my ear. Repeating what she had first done.

The host seated us at a corner booth, forcing us to sit side by side. I wondered if she planned it that way. I wondered if she had any idea how much I had planned for the evening. I had spent the previous three days trying on dozens of dresses, buying new pink-red lingerie (raspberry), and deciding which color lipstick she would like most. Naturally I chose Raspberry Danish. I unbuttoned my very practical beige raincoat, taking a little extra time before opening it up. Her first comment was "Wow." I was wearing a beautiful low-cut sapphire dress with a thick slash of metallic silver down one breast and around my waist, trailing down my butt. I turned so she could see the shining zipper down the back. "You look so fu–" She didn't finish the sentence because the wait staff arrived with a whiskey.

"I'm a regular," she told me. They knew her drink, but I didn't know mine. I asked Marti what I should have, and all she did was laugh. I was put off. It was rude to laugh at me. I ordered a white wine. I hadn't even sat down. She took my coat and tossed it to the far end of the booth, on top of her leather jacket. She touched my waist to move me in, and I melted into the booth. I instantly forgot and forgave her rudeness. She pressed herself in beside me. Her heat warmed my chilled bones. She took a deep breath in and said "Wow," again. She wasn't looking at my eyes, but my cleavage when she said that. It made the expense of the new bra totally worth it.

I reached into my purse and pulled out my Raspberry Danish lipstick. I locked eyes with her, uncapped the lipstick and turned the tube. A rich pink-red rose up. I think I heard her moan. "I don't have a mirror. Can you do my lipstick?" I handed the tube to her, looked into her eyes and formed my lips in a soft O. She watched my lips move as she slowly applied my lipstick. She leaned in close to me and said, "I need to kiss you. Can I kiss you?" I could feel her desire grow as I counted to three before I closed my lips and replied, "Yes." She kissed me and a shock shot straight through my spine. She kept her lips pressed on to mine. Harder, then softer, in a rhythm my pussy started to pulse to. I heard the soft thunk of my wine glass arriving, but I couldn't pull myself from her. Only she had the strength to separate us. It felt like she pulled my core out.

The wait staff came back and efficiently presented the menu, then disappeared again. "I like it here," Marti said, "because the staff are discreet and friendly." I hadn't seen their friendliness yet. I suppose that allowing us to kiss in the booth was the discreet part. "I need to kiss you again." From the way she said it, I was doubtful it was going to be the type of kiss a restaurant would appreciate. She kissed me anyway, hard and deep. Her hand slipped around my waist and down to the uppermost of my ass. I felt dizzy. When she pulled back and I opened my eyes, the wait staff was back.

"You eat meat?" I wasn't sure if that was a question or a command. I told her I was open, but that I'd enjoy whatever she chose.

"You choose."

I looked over the menu quickly. "Tawa and Keema."

"What's that?"

"Tawa Bread Rolls are spiced vegetables rolled in bread and then shallow-fried on a griddle. Great paired with a spicy chutney. Chicken Keema is minced spiced chicken rolled in bread, and then fried."

"Never had either of them here. They sound like something a baker would like."

"Good thing I'm a baker then." The wait staff took the order and disappeared.

"Your breasts are beautiful." It was completely unexpected. I have to admit, when she said that, my pussy got another little shock. I looked around to see who might have heard her, but I don't think anyone did. The only blushing face was mine.

The food arrived. Sharing plates with Marti was unnerving, but I put that on me. She eats with gusto. Verve. She savors and smacks and snatched food from right under my hand. She thinks it's funny. At one point, she grabbed my fingers and licked off a spot of chutney. Her boldness is natural for her.

We got to talking about books. Marti used to be a voracious reader. That does not surprise me. She seems to devour everything in her path. Once she set her eye on it, one way or another, it would be hers. Like me.

I prefer contemporary authors like Degus and Goldstein, but she likes the old noir mysteries, like Hammett and Chandler. "I loved holding an actual paperback book sitting in bed, drinking a whiskey and reading about Sam Spade and Philip Marlowe," she said. She downed the last of her whiskey and the wait staff showed up instantly with a new one.

"I think Degus's novel 'Lance's Fractured Realities,' is one of the best murder mystery series ever written. I'm pretty sure that he travels back to the 1930s just so he can work with Marlowe."

"I doubt Marlowe knew him."

"I'd recommend it. Book 7, I think."

"I just don't think Marlowe would agree to work with anyone. Never mind a guy named Lance."

"That's the nice things about fiction. The author controls everything."

"I doubt Marlowe would agree with that, either. Besides, Degus's theory of time travel was the 'Quantum Echo Theory,' which is bullshit."

"Why is it bullshit? The idea that every action or event leaves behind a quantum echo, sounds reasonable to me. You harness the imprint in the fabric of spacetime to traverse backward or forward in time."

"We can't manipulate quantum entanglement at a macroscopic scale, so even if these echoes exist, we could never find and exploit them."

"How much do you know about quantum entanglement theory?"

"More than Degus, I would say."

"What about quantum entanglement to instantaneously teleport objects or information across vast distances?"

"In fiction, sure. But in real life? It violates fundamental principles of causality and relativity, and disregards the conservation of energy and the no-communication theorem."

"If you're this smart, why are you a private investigator and not a quantum physicist?"

"No one wants to fuck a quantum physicist. But I get pussy for days as a P.I. And before you ask, yes, it is worth it."

I asked why she became a private investigator, other than all the women throwing themselves at her feet. She said a lot of former police go into investigation or security. Then she asked me why I became a baker. I was a little uneasy telling her.

The store was originally owned by Li Chen and Zhao Shuang. I'd been working at the bakery for a few years, and we'd always gotten along well. It wasn't a passion, it was a nice job. That's all. Then they sold me the bakery–lock, stock, and barrel–for next to nothing. They'd read the political writing on the wall. Within days of getting all the paperwork signed and registered, the government began mass expropriation of Chinese-owned land in America. They left the week before the three-day US-China war started. I kept paying them until it became illegal to send money to anyone in China. The war was over by the time the law came in, but it's still in effect. Marti said she lost a secretary to the Expulsion Act that followed.

Writing any more about that might get me arrested.

We talked about the bakery. After Marti's dramatic arrest, the bakery became popular with social media wannabees who were hoping to live stream a dramatic repeat. When they petered out, crime podcasters filled the seats. At least they bought food without me first threatening to kick them out. That lasted a year, and then things returned to normal. I was grateful. I don't want publicity, I want sales.

"I can always bust through the door and break a few windows again."

"Someone did start breaking in and taking the day-after-day-olds. Nothing else. They somehow got in and out through the ceiling. I never figured out how. And I live above the bakery. I decided to put the day-afters outside on a table. And that seemed to work really well. No more break-ins. Security footage showed a few people would take one or two things, leave some for someone else."

"You're an angel."

"Mmm. Someone has taken to peeing on the food and ruining it. I just see someone in a hoodie on the video."

"Call the cops?" It was my turn to laugh. "You're doing such a nice thing. I bet it changes soon. They'll get bored."

"I hope so. The only benefit of the constant rain we have is that I don't have to wash the sidewalk down afterwards."

Chapter Three

Dinner wound down, and we skipped the dessert menu. Marti'd had a few whiskeys, while I stuck with my single glass of wine. She lit up a cigarette and blew the smoke away from me. All those years of anti-smoking became meaningless when Morris became president and outlawed banning smoking. At least the tobacco companies had figured out how to create a cigarette paper that removed almost all the bad stuff. Smokers still had a distinctive "fuck you" attitude when they lit up. And I told her that. "That's a very strong 'fuck you' statement you're sending me," I said. She softened her eyes and replied, "All night long. Unless you have someone to get home to?"

"No one. I wouldn't be here if I had a girlfriend. Do you have a girlfriend?" She just shrugged and said, "A few. But you're the one I'm here with tonight." I was okay with that. When the wait staff brought the bill, Marti quickly tapped and paid for everything. I argued for a moment about splitting the bill, but she said I could pay it off by letting her have a little extra fun tonight.

"What kind of fun?"

"Where will you put this? Right now?" She held her hand up just below table level. I looked around to see if anyone was watching. Of course they weren't. It was just us paying attention to us. I bit my lower lip and my fingers shook a little as I reached up and pulled her hand down to my lap. Her skin was rough on my skin as she slipped between my legs and stroked the inside of my thigh. I quivered. She moved her hand up until her fingers were touching me through my panties. "Silk." My head spun. She rubbed me a little more, then one finger made its way past the gusset and she stroked me a few times before withdrawing from me. I'm certain there had been fireworks somewhere. She put her elbow on the table and her chin in her hand and drew a deep breath. "Lavender. Bergamot." She stared at me as she licked her finger a few times. "You'll appreciate this one: Tahitian vanilla," she said. In contrast to Vanilla planifolia, Tahitian vanilla is renowned for its delicate, fruity taste profile. It has hints of cherry, anise, and a subtle touch of licorice.

Marti loved describing the flavors of women. Her opinion of me inspired me to create some very delicious cookies. They're a best-seller at the bakery. The scent of sugar always lingers in the air here. The Tahitian vanilla is a sweet reminder of my indulgent secret.

It didn't seem like much to her, but for me, it was a first. I'd never had anyone touch me like that in public, and I was a little wobbly when we stood up to leave. I was thankful the silver on my dress was already shiny. My wetness wasn't obvious. Once my coat was on, I relaxed a little more. She put on her jacket and I got a better look at it.

I tapped a hole in the side and teased her about it. She moved her arm and asked me to put my finger in it. I knew it wouldn't be dirty, it was just a hole in the side of the jacket. So I put my little finger through the hole. When she told me to press a little further, I did. I could feel a small bump under her shirt. It was a bullet wound, she explained.

As we slowly walked toward her apartment on Raven-scrook–she lived in the aptly named Blightwood neigh-borhood–she told me about the wound. She'd been hired to find a young man and was tailing a low-level drug dealer who she thought had information on him. He round-ed the corner, and she followed without caution. Drunk, she said. The dealer was waiting for her. Shot her. Fled. She ran after him, because of course she would. She's still very fit for a woman with so many addictions. She ran after the dealer, caught up and tripped him. After some persuasion–she didn't go into detail–he told her where to find the man she was looking for. She found him. He wanted nothing to do with his family, and that was that. She went to a nearby walk-in AutoMedi, had a bot remove the bullet and called the family to tell them their son was alive but wanted no contact. AutoMedis aren't known for their aesthetic work. Her scar was noticeable.

I asked if she has ever shot someone. "Of course. Haven't you?" I thought she was serious, but she started laughing and said she'd shot but never killed anyone. "I've never even critically wounded anyone. I've been shot more than I've done the shooting."

"That seems odd for a police officer."

"Homicide detective. It would be antithetical, don't you think? I know the police don't have a stellar reputa-tion–"

"To say the least."

"But there were enough murders to solve without me raising the stats. Do you have scars?"

"Only one from a childhood accident. Fell off my bike."

"Sounds almost idyllic."

"Almost." I did have an almost idyllic childhood. My parents were great at keeping me safe in a very unsafe world. Imagine my sense of betrayal when I found out the truth. Found out places like Falls City existed with neighborhoods like Blightwood. One of the most noto-rious and unsafest residential areas. Once a thriving com-munity, Blightwood had fallen far. Even foreign real estate investors stayed away now.

Run-down stores, vacant lots overgrown with weeds, and graffiti-covered highrises.

Gunfire is a more common sound than police sirens. I put my arm through Marti's. She felt powerful and wild. I felt safer.

Chapter 3

Dinner wound down, and we skipped the dessert menu. Marti'd had a few whiskeys, while I stuck with my single glass of wine. She lit up a cigarette and blew the smoke away from me. All those years of anti-smoking became meaningless when Morris became president and outlawed banning smoking. At least the tobacco companies had figured out how to create a cigarette paper that removed almost all the bad stuff. Smokers still had a distinctive "fuck you" attitude when they lit up. And I told her that. "That's a very strong 'fuck you' statement you're sending me," I said. She softened her eyes and replied, "All night long. Unless you have someone to get home to?"

"No one. I wouldn't be here if I had a girlfriend. Do you have a girlfriend?" She just shrugged and said, "A few. But you're the one I'm here with tonight." I was okay with that. When the wait staff brought the bill, Marti quickly tapped and paid for everything. I argued for a moment about splitting the bill, but she said I could pay it off by letting her have a little extra fun tonight.

"What kind of fun?"

"Where will you put this? Right now?" She held her hand up just below table level. I looked around to see if anyone was watching. Of course they weren't. It was just us paying attention to us. I bit my lower lip and my fingers shook a little as I reached up and pulled her hand down to my lap. Her skin was rough on my skin as she slipped between my legs and stroked the inside of my thigh. I quivered. She moved her hand up until her fingers were touching me through my panties. "Silk." My head spun. She rubbed me a little more, then one finger made its way past the gusset and she stroked me a few times before withdrawing from me. I'm certain there had been fireworks somewhere. She put her elbow on the table and her chin in her hand and drew a deep breath. "Lavender. Bergamot." She stared at me as she licked her finger a few times. "You'll appreciate this one: Tahitian vanilla," she said. In contrast to Vanilla planifolia, Tahitian vanilla is renowned for its delicate, fruity taste profile. It has hints of cherry, anise, and a subtle touch of licorice.

Marti loved describing the flavors of women. Her opinion of me inspired me to create some very delicious cookies. They're a best-seller at the bakery. The scent of sugar always lingers in the air here. The Tahitian vanilla is a sweet reminder of my indulgent secret.

It didn't seem like much to her, but for me, it was a first. I'd never had anyone touch me like that in public, and I was a little wobbly when we stood up to leave. I was thankful the silver on my dress was already shiny. My wetness wasn't obvious. Once my coat was on, I relaxed a little more. She put on her jacket and I got a better look at it.

I tapped a hole in the side and teased her about it. She moved her arm and asked me to put my finger in it. I knew it wouldn't be dirty, it was just a hole in the side of the jacket. So I put my little finger through the hole. When she told me to press a little further, I did. I could feel a small bump under her shirt. It was a bullet wound, she explained.

As we slowly walked toward her apartment on Ravenscrook–she lived in the aptly named Blightwood neighborhood–she told me about the wound. She'd been hired to find a young man and was tailing a low-level drug dealer who she thought had information on him. He rounded the corner, and she followed without caution. Drunk, she said. The dealer was waiting for her. Shot her. Fled. She ran after him, because of course she would. She's still very fit for a woman with so many addictions. She ran after the dealer, caught up and tripped him. After some persuasion–she didn't go into detail–he told her where to find the man she was looking for. She found him. He wanted nothing to do with his family, and that was that. She went to a nearby walk-in AutoMedi, had a bot remove the bullet and called the family to tell them their son was alive but wanted no contact. AutoMedis aren't known for their aesthetic work. Her scar was noticeable.

I asked if she has ever shot someone. "Of course. Haven't you?" I thought she was serious, but she started laughing and said she'd shot but never killed anyone. "I've never even critically wounded anyone. I've been shot more than I've done the shooting."

"That seems odd for a police officer."

"Homicide detective. It would be antithetical, don't you think? I know the police don't have a stellar reputation–"

"To say the least."

"But there were enough murders to solve without me raising the stats. Do you have scars?"

"Only one from a childhood accident. Fell off my bike."

"Sounds almost idyllic."

"Almost." I did have an almost idyllic childhood. My parents were great at keeping me safe in a very unsafe world. Imagine my sense of betrayal when I found out the truth. Found out places like Falls City existed with neighborhoods like Blightwood. One of the most notorious and unsafest residential areas. Once a thriving community, Blightwood had fallen far. Even foreign real estate investors stayed away now.

Run-down stores, vacant lots overgrown with weeds, and graffiti-covered highrises.

Gunfire is a more common sound than police sirens. I put my arm through Marti's. She felt powerful and wild. I felt safer.

Chapter 4

Marti's building was a fifth-floor walk-up, as decrepit as the others in the area. A man stood at the doorway and when he saw her, he held the door open for her. She shook his hand and stepped through, me following closely behind. "Did you just tip him?" I saw her give him money on that handshake. She held out her hand, a metal Shadow inhaler in the palm. "Just doing business." I asked if she was going to get high tonight. "No. It's for another time." I believed her.

She lit a cigarette and we walked up to her apartment. I was shocked at the crumbling walls but the clean stairwell. The hallway was the same. No garbage, no one sleeping or passed out. But the drywall was marred and decayed in places where wallpaper had been ripped off. Which was most places. It looked to me to be a shabbier version of the places I'd lived while going to college. Those places were broke. This place was poor.

"It's small," she said as she unlocked the door. It was. A studio with enough room for a bed, a bistro table, two chairs, and not much more. She had expanded her living space out the window, where a chair sat on the metal fire escape. She moved here just after leaving the force, when her income prospects were bad. Now that they were good, "excellent sometimes," she stayed. She loved the area, the bodega down the street that sold her brands of cigarettes and whiskey, and the park nearby. She loved the easy and safe access to drugs.

It had a hominess to it I really liked. The bed was crisply clean, the apartment a little less so. But nothing else lived there. A nice leather case sat open on the floor by her bed, holding a humble selection of sex toys. She had a toaster and a countertop air fryer. The windows could use a clean, but every window in Falls City could do with the same. The fire escape was gated off to stop any would-be thieves, and probably prevent escape in case of fire. A book reader sat on the table. A gift from a librarian, she said. The air was clean and fresh: a sure sign she'd been expecting me to come home with her.

She threw her jacket over the back of a chair and offered to take my coat. I was surprised when she opened a portion of the wall, revealing a tiny closet. Everything hung front ways rather than sideways.

Watching her pull the drapes shut made me excited. We were almost there. It had been a long time for me. As she approached me, she unbuttoned her shirt. No bra. Flesh. Her breasts were small and stayed coyly hidden by her white shirt. Two small vertical, mismatched scars, well-healed and flesh-colored, ran down her stomach. She breathed with her entire body. Pulsed. She kissed me, pressing herself against me before pulling back and looking at me. I was staring into the eyes of a lion, a meat eater. She was going to eat me alive.

She kissed me again, her lips more insistent this time. Her tongue made its way along my lips, then pushed in. My breath hitched. She stepped back again. This time, she spun me around. Wrapping her arms around my waist, she leaned close to my ear. Kissed my neck. One hand left my waist and the zipper on the back of the dress descended.

"What do you like?"

"Everything." The moment that word left my lips, I panicked. I knew my 'everything' was nowhere near the same as her 'everything.' She must have felt my body tense up.

"Well, let's take 'everything' slow. Maybe stick with a few basics tonight." I instantly melted. She knew, and I knew she cared. Over time, she made me comfortable saying words and saying what I want from sex. I came to like the words 'pussy,' 'breasts,' and 'ass'. I like the words 'yes,' 'there,' and 'don't move.' I learned to be specific. And to stop using words like 'everything' and 'everywhere' because, in fact, I don't like everything, and I don't like everywhere.

She kissed me again as she stood behind me, holding my dress up. I didn't want it on the floor, so I took it over to her hidden closet and hung it up. When I turned around, she was right there. She'd snuck up, cat-like, and startled me. "Your bra and panties are a wonderful color." She stroked my breasts, tracing her fingers along the fabric. "I need to touch your skin." I nodded, but she waited until I said 'yes' before she slipped her fingers under the bra, grazing my nipples. She ran her fingers in small circles, confined by the fabric until she made her way behind me. She unclasped my bra and kissed my shoulders as the thin straps fell away. She cupped my breasts and kissed my neck.

I got light-headed as her hands moved down my belly. She pulled me closer to her and let one hand make its way between my legs. She smoothed my panties down. She brought her hand up and pressed in. I shivered and felt a surge. She felt my dampness and withdrew just enough to come around the front. She took my hand, turning it so it went between my legs and my fingers were brushing my wet pussy. I drew a sharp breath.

She kissed me and hooked her fingers into the elastic waistband, then moved her entire body down mine as she pulled my panties down. She was on her knees in front of me. I put my hand on her shoulder to steady myself as I lifted one leg to step out of the last of my lingerie. When I lifted my other leg, she took hold of my foot and raised it a little higher. She lowered it onto the edge of the bed.

I almost collapsed when I realized I was spread wide open to her gaze.

She kissed the insides of my thighs, then moved to the middle, kissing and licking up every drop I was offering. She has a magnificent talent with her lips and tongue. I don't think my pussy has ever been so passionately kissed. Like a long-lost lover returning from the sea. Or so I imagine. She held my waist to keep me in place, available. My orgasm was building, and she knew it. She would take me to the edge, then back off for a moment, and take me to the edge again. I thought she was making gasping sounds, but it was me. I quivered and moaned, held her head in both hands, fingers gripping her hair. She brought me to the edge again, and this time, pushed me over. My orgasm went on and on as she sucked every drop from me.

"Lie down," she said as she pushed my hips back. I fell willingly on the bed, still gasping for air. "You're delicious. I'm going to keep eating all night long!" I thought I would black out from pleasure first. I was so weak and she was so impatient. She grabbed my ankles and swung my legs onto the bed so I was now lying in the middle. Then she built a pillow fort around me. A pillow under my head and back, and one under my hips to raise me up more. She pushed my legs so they bent and rested on more pillows. And she settled in.

She kissed my belly and moved onto my mons, stroking my hair before pressing in with her mouth. She worked all around my clit, and would ask, "more?" and I would say "Yes, more."

She slowly licked from the top to the bottom, splitting my lips on the way down. Then she took one long stroke up from my fourchette, through my slit and up to my clit, where she circled around. Down, and the second stroke up was slower, pressing my lips apart. She lightly swiped her tongue across my clit, just grazing it. I started to tremble as her tongue went down a third time. Up again and when she got to my clit, she paused and gently pressed her tongue directly on my clit. And then she let go, licking and sucking and kissing and pulling. That beautiful sensation came over me and I orgasmed.

She laid for a moment with her face pressed into my pussy before she pulled up. She straddled my hips, and I feel her damp heat against my belly. I was still trying to catch my breath. She leaned back a little, presenting herself. "Finger me," she demanded. I fondled her with pleasure. I was at first self-conscious, aware I wasn't nearly as proficient or skilled. But within minutes, she was coming on my stomach. As she orgasmed in my hands, I knew I was good enough and almost cried.

Marti moved off of me and back between my legs. She used her fingers to stroke and her tongue to lick. I climaxed quickly, but the waves just kept flowing, rocking me over and over. I was quaking, but she wasn't done with me.

She sank her fingers into my aching, wet pussy. I didn't think my clit could handle more, but it didn't matter. She curled two fingers inside and stroked my G-spot, bringing me to orgasm again. Then she was done. She kissed my pussy one last time and hiked herself up and over all the pillows. She laid down beside me and pulled me onto her. I was sweating, my forehead tucked into her neck. I let my weight press on her. She pulled me closer, one hand on the small of my back, the other on my butt.

"Grab the duvet," she said after a few quiet moments. I pulled up the cover while she sent most of the pillows flying to the floor. She stayed flat on her back while I cuddled under her arm. I could smell her sweet sweat. I discovered a few months later, the sweetness was the drug she took, coming out with her sweat. I fell easily asleep.

I awoke alone. I found Marti sitting in the single chair on the fire escape, smoking. "Grab the duvet and come on out." I protested as the duvet would get wet and dirty. She laughed and said it is always getting wet and dirty. When she said those last two words, I felt a little jolt of pleasure. I wrapped myself in the duvet and wiggled my way out the window. She patted her lap, and I obediently sat down, shifting my legs until I felt safely cradled.

She flicked her cigarette butt into the night. The embers glowed down and out of sight. Reaching down beside her, she retrieved a shot glass, offering me whiskey. I politely declined. She took a sip as I settled my head against her.

The glow of neon from below created stunning slivers of light on wet metal. We were there long enough for her to take a hit of Shadow and for me to fall asleep in her arms.

Chapter 5

I woke up when she started shivering beneath me. It scared me and I struggled to wake her. Finally awake, sort of, I helped her back inside, to the bed. There was nowhere else to go. "I'm fine, I'm fine," she said in a way that made me think she probably was fine. She probably was used to taking too much. I wasn't. I'd seen it only once before, and only the aftermath.

I went to my brother's home. A rundown little place, smaller even than this. My parents had called and said they couldn't reach him. I told them it was nothing, but you know how parents can be. I took the bus; I doubted a car would survive the ordeal. The heavy glass front door to the building has a spiderweb crack in it about head height. It was there when Don moved in.

When I walked in, there was a hallway to apartments, and a stairway on the right. Don was on three, and I start up. I hate the smell of this place; urine, feces, vomit. I put on a medical face mask I've carried in my pocket for a year. It does nothing to stop the smell, but now I am less worried about catching some airborne disease. The walls were once covered in artistic graffiti, but the artists left. There are gang tags spray painted over the art. But even the gangs are gone. Over the gang tags there are cryptic words placed there by people who have lost their minds to drugs. Rarely is there sense to any of it.

I put my key into the lock, and it clicked. "At least it's locked," I thought. Every day I would look at his key on my ring, the key with the yellow cap. I hated having it. It was given to me by my parents, who live across the country. I lived in the same city. I can take the key and keep an eye on him. "Don? You home?" I called through open the door. No answer meant I had to step in. "Don?" Silence. I walk in and let the door shut behind me.

It's a one-room studio. He's not here. On the table is a sandwich, half eaten. Cheese and butter. His favorite. The bread is out; the cheese cracking as it dried. There are empty beer cans in the corner, empty packets of sugar on the counter. An addict's snack. Don was alright for the first year on his own, but in Falls City life doesn't get easier or more forgiving. If you fall, no one is there for you. And Don fell. Hard and fast. He fell in love with heroin the very first time he tried it.

"Don?"

The only other room in the apartment is the bathroom. I don't want to go in. "Don? Are you on the can? Don?" I shake as I turn the handle and open the door. Don is there.

He is slumped between the toilet and the wall. His eyes are open. I can't quite understand what I'm seeing. I bend down and wave my hands in front of his face to get his attention. "Don?" He's not moving. One arm is across his chest, the other sits straight on his lap. There's a needle in it, just hanging there. I tapped his cheek to wake him, but it felt cold and stiff against my fingertip. His lips are blue. His eyes are voids. I leaped backwards, screaming "ohfuckohfuckohfuck!" and slam my back against the edge of the door frame.

I flew out of the bathroom and dug into my pockets for my phone. I dropped it again before I could dial all three numbers. I skittered on the floor after it. "Police, fire or medical?" Medical? Maybe a priest to resurrect him. I tell them where I am, but I have to leave. I can't be in the same room with him. With the door open, it has become one room. No, I can't give CPR. He is cold and blue and his skin is stiff. I vomit. They are 4 minutes away.

An old man sticks his head in the doorway. He is not a paramedic. He is a neighbor. "Is Don okay?" No. Absolutely not okay. The man steps in, looks through the bathroom door, and guides me into the hallway. "Best to wait here," he said. The paramedics came up the stairs huffing and puffing, then cram their bulk through the apartment door and into the bathroom. It's too small. They drag Don out by his ankles. He remains in that seated position. The only thing to be done for him was to give him a decent funeral.

"Got any juice?" I asked Marti. I'm thirsty and I need sweet and shocking. Apple juice would be perfect. "Orange juice in the fridge. Get some for me too. Please?" I found three of every type of dinnerware: three bowls, three plates, three cups, three glasses. I asked why they were in threes, not fours. She often had couples over, but very rarely thruples. I brought two large glasses of juice to the bed.

She was sitting up, much more awake than dead, and drank some juice.

"That was a lot."

"Of juice?"

"Of drugs."

"I had some Shadow."

"You did."

"That wasn't a lot. It's a measured dose. After hours of fucking, I was tired. Don't hold that against Shadow."

That was fair. I was tired too. Exhausted. It was 3:43am. I needed the sugar from the juice and took a big gulp. After half a glass, I felt more like myself; we fell asleep much more comfortably in bed.

The sun actually broke through the clouds and shone in my eyes, waking me. I gently prodded Marti, but all she did was turn away from me. I tried again, and she scooched backwards until she pressed against me. One more time, and she took hold of my hand and put it on her breast. I gave her nipple a quick squeeze and padded off to the tiny bathroom. When I walked out of the shower, I found she was gone.

I have seen movies and read books where the romantic interest leaves their new partner in their home, and I always wondered how the last person locks the door when they leave. Do I hunt for a key? Climb out the window? Leave it unlocked? Hope it's an auto lock?

Maybe she'd gone out for a smoke and is expecting to find me when she returns. I was surprised she didn't want more sex. I know I'm not the best in bed, but am I bad enough that you leave your own place rather than speak to me? My doubts were getting the better of me.

The only difference between a locked and an unlocked door is someone trying the handle. There was nothing I could do. I got dressed and went to work. I left the door unlocked. My staff was there. They had done all the morning's baking and opened the shop without me. Grace has a key. When I walked in, she gave me a look and laughed. I was still wearing my very beautiful dress. I felt defiant. I put my apron on and got to work. Grace asked if I was alright: I was never late to open the store. There was a lot of teasing between the loaves of sourdough and cherry tarts.

"Come on, tell us who it is." Grace starts to chant, "Tell us. Tell us. Tell us." I'm serving a customer who wants to hear what I have to say. I turn my head, shoot a STFU look, and serve the customer. But once the coast is clear, Jean joins in.

"Man or woman or neither?"

"Or both?"

I've only ever slept with women, and only two. Now three. I don't want to talk about it too much because being inexperienced ends up feeling more like a fetish and less like the truth. Neither Grace nor Jean know. Of course. For as jokey as things can get, I am the boss.

"Stop it!" I say, but lightheartedly. I kind of want to talk about Marti.

"Talk. Talk. Talk."

I grinned when I thought of kissing her. "She's a great kisser."

"I knew it! Is she tall?"

"Taller than me." I'm not good at judging height. If I have to look up, you're tall. If I have to really crane my neck, you're still tall.

"Almost everyone is taller than you."

"Thanks."

"Blonde? Brunette?"

"Oh! A hot redhead!"

"Black hair."

"Is it dyed?" Jean is trying to trick me into saying whether I've seen her naked. "She's blushing! The woman is a natural."

"Name?"

"No."

"You didn't get her name?" That set both of them off, hooting so loudly the customer looks over. Enviously.

"Of course I have her name. We actually met years ago."

"What? No. Who?"

"You don't know her." It's entirely possible one or both could know her. But neither worked here when Marti made her mad entrance.

"I might know her…actually, no. I don't know any black-haired woman who are good kissers."

"Are women with black hair brunettes?"

"No, brunettes have brown hair."

"What do you call black haired women?"

Jean looked up the answer and incredulously said, "Brunette."

"Did you go out somewhere nice?"

"A restaurant. The Findlay."

"How was it?"

They were asking a lot of questions and wanted more than the answers I was giving. I want to say more. I want to say she was gorgeous and hot. I want to say she fingered me in a public restaurant and it was wild and wet. I want to say she created a pillow nest and ate me for hours. I want to say she came in my hands.

I told them she'd kissed me and said I tasted like lavender, Tahitian vanilla and bergamot. They were thrilled with the idea of developing a new cookie. I told them we fell asleep outside in a chair, cuddling under a duvet. They thought it was romantic. And it was.

When I finally got things organized and felt comfortable, I headed into my office and called Sandy. I can tell her almost anything.

Chapter 6

Almost two weeks later, just past noon, I was in the basement when Grace came in with a smile on her face. "I think your black-haired woman is here." I had been tending my mycelium. Two years ago, the federal government abandoned their bio-engineered mycelium program. Through genetic and synthetic engineering, they created a hyper-palatable mushroom that was so nutrient dense it could end hunger in the country. It turned out, the big companies that developed it weren't interested in the project's final product, only in the development money. No one could make money off slow-growing, tasty, healthy mushrooms, and the project was abandoned to NGOs. I had signed up with one and was growing mushrooms in the basement. And it was damned slow.

I headed upstairs and looked out of the kitchen. There she is, at a table, with a coffee in one hand and a cigarette in the other. Her leather jacket was hanging on the back of the chair. She was slouching, her legs spread out. A little shock went through me when I saw her. Grace and Jean were almost as excited as I was. "Her nipples are hard. She's glad to see you."

"Or she's cold…No. She's glad to see me." I winked, leaving them both agape behind the counter, and joined Marti at the table. Her nipples were hard and beautiful under the thin cloth of her t-shirt. I didn't even think to take my apron off.

"I've been thinking of you. Where have you been?"

"I can't tell you. It's work related. Confidential."

"Confidential private investigator work?"

"No. Confidential quantum physicist work."

"Undercover?"

"Mmm." She looked at me, licked her lips, and made me wet. "I was hired by a local casino. They knew something was up. Hired me to find out what."

She and her secretary, Susan, went to a local casino and spent a week gambling, fucking and getting high. By the end of the week, she discovered Susan had not only developed a gambling addiction, but had stolen $500,000 from the business account to fund it.

"That's a lot of money."

"No shit. I trusted her with the company's finances. I had her arrested. It was a mess. I have a new policy. No more fucking my secretaries."

"Did you get your money back?"

"Oh no. The casino wasn't going to cover my loss just because I was working for them. But it worked out. A day after Susan's arrest, a floor runner approached me, said I could make my money back." Apparently, word had spread at the casino about Marti's big loss.

A trio of employees—a custodian, a floor runner and a surveillance officer—were working together. They would track down big losers and offer a 40/60 split to game the roulette wheel. The loser got the 40%, they got 60%. Every morning, when fewer people were around, the surveillance officer would train a camera on a different wheel. The custodian would attach two magnets under the table to control the wheel. The floor runner would recruit a gambler to play the wheel.

From their office, the surveillance officer would use AI and a super fast computer to track the ball on the wheel then slow the wheel down with the magnets in a way that, more often than not, would land on the number they wanted—where the gambler had bet. The floor runner would watch for anyone who saw something fishy and tell the officer to stop gaming the wheel until the threat passed.

By using different wheels, different croupiers and different gamblers, they'd gone uncaught for more than a year. The casino boss knew something was going on, but no one knew how it worked or who was involved. The thieves made the mistake of recruiting Marti. She reported them to management and made 250 crisp. Half of what Susan had lost.

"That seems very clever."

"Fucking brilliant. Since everyone involved was breaking the law, no one was ratting to the police. Your employee is heading this way. I'm going to embarrass you."

"What do you–"

"…You moved like that. It made me come so hard." As she said that, she slowly moved her gaze from me to Jean. "She's amazing, you know."

"Hi." Jean stood still, like a deer in headlights. "Is this tantalizing delight for me?" Marti said it in her best sexy voice. I was turned on, and I had to assume Jean was. Jean stood, mouth open, staring into Marti's eyes. I took the plate from Jean, and she left.

I know my cheeks were red. "Do you do that often?"

"All the time. It's funny. You can tell who is going to think it's hot and who is going to be scandalized."

"And which is Jean?"

"Aroused. She will never look at you the same way. Now you're sexual." She lit another cigarette. Normally I don't allow smoking. But it is perversely seductive watching her put it between her lips and suck. And I like to be perversely seduced by her.

I looked quickly around and in a soft voice said, "Tell me something sexual." That got her attention. She picked up the cookie and was about to take a bite, but she paused. She was looking at me. A slow smile creeped across her face. She inhaled deeply.

"Lavender, bergamot."

"Tahitian vanilla icing."

She knew exactly what she was doing to turn me on. She closed her eyes, holding the cookie to her lips. She licked the icing. "Mmm. Sweet." She looked at me and slowly licked the icing again. She parted her lips and slipped the cookie in. Not too far. She closed her lips around it, sucked for a moment, then snapped a tiny piece off. She ran her tongue around her mouth, making a noise that barely escaped her closed lips. "I want to eat this all day long."

I swallowed hard. When she asked me to talk sexually to her, I swallowed harder. I wasn't very good at it. She put the cookie down, put her chin in her hand, and looked at me through hooded eyes.

"You make me feel creamy."

"Like mushroom soup?"

"No. I...I want you to suckle my breasts."

"Suckle? Like a piglet?" She was laughing at me now.

"Oh God, stop it. I can't do it."

"Yes, you can. It's easy. The sexiest thing is to make a woman laugh. You've got me hooked. Try again. Just stay away from barnyard animals."

"You make me wet myself."

She howled and smacked the table. "I'm not into piss."

"That's not what I meant."

"Adjective, not verb. In 'wet myself' it's a verb. In 'make me wet', it is an adjective."

"Thanks for the English lesson."

"I'm a quantum physicist and an English professor. Look at me. Are you wearing underwear?"

I clenched and shifted in my seat. "Yes."

"Now ask me."

"Are you wearing underwear?"

"Let me check." I could hear the soft movement of metal and fabric as she unzipped her jeans. Her hand moved below table level, then she zipped up again. "You tell me." She held her hand out across the table. I didn't dare take my eyes off her for fear of breaking the spell.

I took her hand and kissed it. I could feel some moisture on my lips. "You aren't."

At that moment, a customer shouted at Grace and our spell was broken. I apologized and said I had to go. She asked if she could come back to see me in a couple of days. I said yes. She stood up, walked around the table, and leaned over me. She kissed me hard, and I could feel myself quiver. As she left, she told the customer to grow the fuck up.

Chapter 7

Over time, I learned a lot from Marti about talking sexily. She had asked me to call and leave her erotic messages. I protested, saying she'd only end up with a voicemail box full of cream of mushroom soup recipes. She convinced me I needed to ease into it, and stick to words I liked, not what I thought she wanted to hear. She would call me every morning and leave a message, asking me to talk about something specific. I'd call her back with an answer in my own words.

"Call and tell me you like my hands."

I spent a good part of the morning thinking about her hands. Their rough skin, strong fingers, confident movements. I became aroused. Not orgasmic, but desirous. "I like when your rough fingers slip under my dress and up my thigh."

"Tell me about my tits."

"I like squeezing and kneading your breasts gently. Your nipples get hard between my fingers when I pinch them."

"When I come over tonight, what is the last thing you're going to kiss before falling asleep?"

That one stumped and aroused me for a few hours. I imagined kissing her lips, nibbling her ears, kissing her breasts or pussy. I imagined an evening of exhausting sex, then tucking myself under her arm, head on her chest, falling asleep. "I'm sleepy from orgasm after orgasm. I lie down beside you, putting my hand between your legs. As I begin to fall asleep, I kiss your breast. You get goosebumps around your areola. I blow on the moisture I've left behind and you shiver."

I talk day in and day out. Owning a bakery, I talk to customers and staff, suppliers, inspectors, people placing large orders. Because it's Falls City, I talk to everyone from busy millionaires to mendicant addicts, hungry children to lonely seniors.

I don't know about your experience, but when I talk, I listen more. Talking about oneself is inherently satisfying, activating brain reward centers akin to those triggered by sex, drugs, and food. It's easy to make people feel good about themselves by letting them talk about themselves. You likely feel the urge to interject and discuss your own interests. After all, you want the same rewards. The key is to resist and concentrate on the other person. Your opportunity will come.

As a business owner, I have to remain professional with my customers. I make up for being impersonal by being emotive. Usually supportive of whatever the customer or supplier is talking about. Your car isn't working today? "Oh no! That's terrible. What are you going to do?" Bob the barista down the street got your coffee order wrong? "How frustrating. How do you take your coffee? I'll make one for you and it will be right." When I chat with people at the shop, I make them feel welcomed, but I don't care much about them. One or two, sure. But most? No.

I know how to talk to strangers, even strangers I know. But it was through Marti that I learned to talk to lovers. It's very different.

When Marti came over one night, I discovered although she isn't much of a talker, she can listen herself into an orgasm. It's amazing to watch her become aroused while I whisper in her ear. Her nipples get hard, her stomach tightens. Without any touch at all, her breath will hitch and her hips will rise and she will spasm as she comes. These aren't monstrous orgasms, but undeniably plea-surable waves. It makes for easy foreplay. I've never met anyone quite like her.

Chapter 8

Marti comes in and out of my life in phases. It seemed the reasons for her absence weren't always work related. I knew she would find a new woman, or women, and hole up with them for a while. Then she would appear in my bakery, or leave a message for me to come to see her. I never made the request for her to come and see me. I couldn't stand the thought that she would not respond. Or worse, that she would say 'no'. But the shop kept me busy. And the neighborhood kept me busy. I was still struggling with my random spoiler who would urinate or defecate on any baked goods I left out.

At the end of every day, I package up individual servings of 2-day-old pastries and bread. A loaf of bread is always the most popular item. I put a lot of effort into putting out the older food. I treat everything with mycelium and wrap them in plastic to keep it dry from rain. Some people make it last a week. From what I've heard from a few locals, minutes after I put out the food and go to my apartment above the bakery, the fiend strikes. I've tried putting out cameras, but he doesn't care. He wears black and has a hood up, so I never see his face. I can't describe him. I've tried reporting it to police but the food I leave out is considered "abandoned property"–garbage–and there's actually no law against crapping on garbage.

One rainy morning, before 5am, I left my apartment. The door is at the back of the building. I walked around the side and was surprised to see absolutely nothing on my display table. I normally find the soiled goods, but this time, nothing. All the items were gone, and there was no telltale pile of feces anywhere. I was perplexed until I rounded the corner to the front of my store.

The entrance has an awning over a double door of PlasGlass, an unbreakable glass replacement. I learned my lesson thanks to Marti. I sometimes find people sleeping here. This morning, I found my fiend. He was asleep in my doorway, turned away from the rain. There were a couple of empty wine bottles close by, and a drug inhaler. Clearly, he had taken too much, and passed out before doing anything to the food. It was the same black clothes, the same hoodie. It was the same guy. Seeing him lying there, blocking my doorway, him having caused so much trouble, I snapped.

I skulked toward him. It was easy to be quiet in the rain. I got right up next to him. He was lying on his side, curled up, his back toward me. One arm was tucked under his head as a pillow. I leaned against the old wood walls of the doorway. I could feel the cracking paint pressing into the palm of my hand, tiny bits of rotten wood crumbling under my fingers. His scent, booze and...something familiar...made it hard to think. I was tempted to turn away, seek help in getting him out of my doorway. But this was my doorway, my bakery, my building. And he wasn't welcome. I wasn't going to be cruel, but I wanted to be firm.

"Get the hell out of here!" I yelled as I kicked him in the ass. He grunted and roused himself. I stepped back, suddenly aware maybe kicking him hadn't been a good idea. He rose up with a surprising fluidity, rubbing his butt. He turned around and glared at me.

"What the fuck did I do?"

It was Marti, and she was both confused and angry.

"I'm so sorry! I didn't know it was you!"

"You go around kicking strangers?"

I tried to explain that I thought she was a homeless guy. I tried to explain I thought she had been urinating on my bread. I tried to explain that I didn't normally go around kicking anyone, whether I know them or not. I stepped toward her and she pushed me away.

"Fuck off."

"I thought you were the guy–"

"I took care of him. He won't be back. For that, I deserve more than a kick in the ass."

"I didn't know."

"You didn't know, so your first thought was kicking a sleeping person?"

"I'm so sorry, Marti. I–"

"Fuck off." And with that, she pushed me aside and stormed off in the rain, sending a bottle skittering as she left. I felt terrible. I called after her, but my voice was lost in the rain. I walked into the shop, sat down at a table, and cried for 20 minutes.

I'm not much of a crier, despite what I just wrote. When my last girlfriend left me–I am not the one who left her–we had been together for 10 years, 5 months, 3 days. She said she'd found someone else. She expected me to beg, cry, shout, scream, argue. She–Deirdre–expected me to cling to her neck, throw myself prostrate and wrap myself around her ankles. I was supposed to protest that only she mattered and not her indiscretions, that I needed her because without her, there was no life, no breath. Deirdre expected me to act as I always acted when she made it known that she found someone younger, smarter, prettier.

Once every couple of years, she would sit down for 'a talk.' She would gleefully list my to-do list: I needed to lose weight, to do something beyond baking, to wear makeup more often, to keep the house cleaner. Of course, this was her to-do list for me, not mine. My to-do list included reading, baking, and standing up for myself. And when she started in on me this last time, I decided to start in on my to-do list.

I didn't want to lose her, but I wondered, what would I actually be losing? Routine? Responsibility? Caring about someone who had grown bored of making love to me? Wanting someone who had stopped wanting me years ago?

There was nothing more I wanted from Deirdre. I didn't want any more of her opinionated blathering. I walked into the bedroom and packed my things. She never came in. She probably thought I was being overly dramatic, although I had never before tried to leave her.

It was something my father taught me: don't threaten it if you aren't willing to do it, and if you're willing to do it, don't wait.

She walked out before I finished, but that made it easier to gather everything from the kitchen. I loaded up the company van and drove to the bakery to sleep in the office. Not a single tear. The next morning, I explained everything to Li and Zhao and they agreed to let me sleep in the office until they moved out of the apartment above the bakery and moved in with their son. I could then have the apartment above the bakery. They swore living with their son was something they always wanted to do. I wasn't going to question my good fortune. Within a week, I was living on my own for the first time in my entire life, in a beautiful big apartment that smelled like cinnamon and yeast. I did not shed a single tear for Deirdre.

Yet here I was, bawling my eyes out over a woman with a body count in the hundreds and a self-serving streak that could put any narcissist to shame.

I called her and left a message, as always. She told me once that she has the phone on silent, with no vibration, but I doubt it. I get the silent part–if you're doing some private investigator work somewhere, you don't want your phone to ring. But the vibration? She's more likely to shove it down her pants than turn it off.

"I'm sorry about what happened. Please call." She didn't. "I'd like to talk to you." No response. "Call me." Nothing. I wasn't sure what to do, so I asked a few friends for their advice about my hypothetical friend. As in, "I have this friend, and she said she screwed up by kicking this woman she's dating, but she thought it was someone else. Now the woman is pissed and won't call. What can my friend do?" Most people just called my friend an abusive asshole and said she didn't deserve anyone. I mean, when you put it that way...

I spoke with Sandy Koldfeld. Sandy and I have been friends for decades, and I'd call and talk to her once or twice a month to see how things are. They were typically boring for her. I told her about my friend's dilemma.

"You kicked someone?" Sandy knew I was talking about myself.

"Not just someone, but a woman I'm kind of seeing."

"Why is this the first time I'm hearing about her?"

"It's very casual." I had to explain that it was a case of mistaken identity. "I don't go around kicking people. But the point isn't that I kicked her, the point is, she's not talking to me."

"No, you're wrong. The point is, you did kick her. And you've already apologized, so don't bother doing that again. Invite her out on a date. Act like, 'Hey, I've apologized, and it's time to move on.' Kevin does that all the time. And don't ask me why, but I let him get away with it. It's just easier, sometimes."

I called her. "Marti, this is Billie. Billie River. This is the last time I'll call you. I'd like to meet you at the Jackaman Art Gallery on Jacob Street, Tuesday night, 8pm. I'll be wearing red until I'm wearing nothing." It sounded sexy when I thought about it. Not so much when I said it. But it was done, and now we had a date. Maybe.

That was four days away. I spent the entire time thinking about which red to wear. I had to consider every detail, every combination, every possibility. Would it be a red dress or a red sweater? Red underwear or dyed red hair. I would spend every morning at the bakery thinking of fashion while I prepared the morning's tarts and buns. She seemed to have a thing for dresses, but I wore a dress every time I saw her. Perhaps something new.

In the afternoons, I would think about how I would take off my clothes if I was lucky enough. Would the dress slide down my body into a mess on the floor? Would the

button by button undoing of my blouse be more arousing? I wouldn't wear socks, but removing hosiery could be
seductive. Did I want my body to be accessible for a quick
fuck, or inaccessible and thus force her to come home with
me?

My nights were spent trying on different combinations
of clothes. Don't let anyone tell you it's not worth spend-
ing time thinking about what to wear. I would try something on, stare and the mirror, and practice taking it off.
How did it feel against my fingers? What was the sound
of the metal clasps coming undone? Could the delicate
material withstand the thick metal zipper on her leather
jacket? If you don't think about dressing for an occasion,
good for you. Marti doesn't. But I do, and if you do, then
I think you understand how exhausting it is to consider all
the possibilities. I fell heavily asleep every night.

I took Tuesday off work, which is quite the rarity. I went
into work to open the safe and prepare the till–it amazes
me that people still use cash as much as they do. But the
rest of the day was mine. I pampered myself with a long,
hot bath. I wanted to smell good for her. I spent a good
part of the afternoon researching the artists whose works
were featured at Jackaman. I had read rave reviews of the
displayed works of Ravenell, Coumbassa and Demeksa,
but I wanted to make sure I would be conversant about
their works and careers. I napped. I ate dinner, although
my stomach was in knots. I prepared myself and hailed a

taxi to the Jackaman gallery. I was blessed it wasn't raining, so I eschewed an overcoat and did not bring an umbrella.

The gallery was a little difficult to find, and the driver became suspicious of me until he finally spotted the neon sign. As one always does in this neighborhood, I paid quickly and got out so the driver could flee. The gallery was below street level, but there were a number of well-dressed affluent patrons and their security guards hovering around the street. Inside, the gallery was crowded. Especially for a Tuesday. Especially for an art gallery in Falls City. When I walked in, I was disappointed that no heads turned. No one thought I looked worthy of paying attention to. Every single woman there was far more glamourous, far more elegant and seductive than I could ever hope to be.

I looked for Marti but didn't see her. It was just after 8pm, and I realized I had no idea if she tended to arrive early or late to an event. Or if she'd even show. So I did what one is supposed to do at an art gallery. I looked at the art. I chatted–with some knowledge now that I'd prepared–about the artists' works and their places in the world of art and politics. I kept looking around, but she hadn't arrived. I was deflated. Hurt. I looked at the time. It was only 8:23pm. I decided I would leave at 8:30pm unless I'd heard from her.

I finally had the opportunity to talk to Mr. Jackaman about the gallery. As we stood conversing before an elegant blue and yellow abstract, she slipped her arms around my waist and pressed herself into my back. "Mind if I steal her away?" Mr. Jackaman just smiled and acquiesced while I melted. She turned me toward the artwork and I wrapped my hands around my waist, holding onto her arms. "I've been watching you." Her words thrilled me, aroused me.

Marti had been at the gallery before me, waiting outside across the street. Waiting for me to arrive. She followed me inside shortly after and proceeded to surveil me. Stalk me. Always just out of my sight, but never out of hers. "I didn't think you'd come," I said. "All over your face," she whispered in my ear. I tensed and clenched and took in a deep breath. She could be so dirty.

I was delighted and disappointed when Mr. Jackaman came back with another visitor and began to chat about Ravenell's impressionist painting before us. She released me and stood next to me, and I was not at all shocked to see that she was looking rough. She was wearing torn jeans and a t-shirt that sat askew under her leather jacket. Her hair was tousled and in her eyes. Her boots were scuffed. She had big silver rings on three fingers, and a necklace with a metal something or other hanging on it. From top to bottom, she looked coarse. Jagged. And the art crowd ate it up. How could they not? She was charismatic, exotic, intelligent. She knew nothing about the art, and everything about letting other people talk. She was high as a kite, and very down to earth. She cast her spell and charmed each one of them, never letting me out of her sight the entire time.

Mr. Jackaman was particularly enthralled, and made a lot of effort to ingratiate himself into our little world of two. "Coumbassa's oeuvre transcends the conventional boundaries of medium and narrative. His distinctive style, characterized by its fusion of drawing and animation, captivates the senses and challenges the intellect. His works are a symphony of contrasts—light and shadow, motion and stillness, chaos and order—each stroke of his brush imbued with a profound sense of purpose and meaning."

She replied, "Imbrication is the visual syntax," and looked at me, as if I had any idea about what she just said. It was not a word I'd read in researching Coumbassa's work. But Mr. Jackaman was delighted by her words.

"Yes, exactly! It is not the paint that overlaps, it is the message that informs his art. His works are a symphony of contrasts—light and shadow, motion and stillness, chaos and order. There is a profound sense of purpose and meaning in each stroke of his brush. Kentridge called his work luminary."

I was amazed people still spoke like this in groups. While Marti and I had joked about physics over dinner, if one is ever to actually joke about physics, talking about visual syntax and messages that inform art? I swear that could get you arrested these days. The art patrons had security guards for a reason.

When Mr. Jackaman finally left us, a couple joined us. They knew Marti as a detective, and thanked her for arresting the killer of their friend, artist Ravyn Carson. She left with them, stepping outside for a cigarette. A grey-haired man approached me and asked if Marti and I would like to join him and his wife–a beautiful brunette standing near a large blue and green Demeksa–after the show. He didn't say what we would be joining them in, but I had an idea. I apologized and said we already had plans. He was disappointed, but gave me his card and asked me to call any time we were available. John Pearce, Antiquities.

When I took his card, his wife came over as if it were a cue. She ran her fingers through my hair and leaned in to kiss me, then stopped with a jerk. Marti grabbed her hair and pulled her back, arching the woman's neck and kissing her violently on the mouth. "That was disappointing." Marti could be so mean sometimes.

John Pearce and his wife were incensed, and promised "so much more." She turned her back on them and kissed me passionately. I could feel her fire down to my toes. She moved us away from the Pearces but it was only minutes later when we were approached by someone else. She looked the woman up and down, then silently shook her head. Dismissed. I had always been the moth, but now I was part of the flame.

It delighted her to play with them like that. They were begging for attention from the one person in the room who knew nothing about the artists, had no interest in having sex with anyone but me, and who helped herself far too much to the free champagne offered by tuxedoed wait staff wandering the crowd.

It was a wonderful evening.

Chapter 9

I thought Marti would be too drunk to have sex that evening. I now realize that's almost possible. She always seems to have the capacity for sex if she wants it. "My place?" I could feel my temperature go up. "Yes?" She said nothing, but took my hand and walked out. The gallery was five blocks from Marti's place, and we walked. We got two blocks before she pulled me into a dark doorway and kissed me. I wondered briefly why we needed to be in the doorway, but when she ran her fingers up my thigh and under my dress, I understood. She squeezed my butt cheeks. "Your underwear feels soft. It must be beautiful." She pushed herself off me and we continued our walk.

We managed two more blocks of dirty murmurs and seductive promises before she stopped again. This time, under a streetlight in the rain, she kissed me and pulled my hand to her breast. I squeezed her nipple and flicked my tongue across her lips. "You excite me. I can feel it all the way to my pussy." I was soaking wet. When I shivered, she put her jacket over my shoulders and we continued on our way.

I was grateful to reach her apartment. "I'm chilled to the bone," I complained. "Make us a couple of whiskeys," she said. I shrugged off her jacket and poured her a drink. I wasn't interested in drinking.

"Not for you?"

"No," I said. I gave her the drink. She took a sip, grimaced, and ran her hand through my wet hair. She grabbed a handful, angled my head back, and kissed me. She pulled my dress up over my hips and grabbed my ass with both hands. She crushed my flesh in her hands, then pulled the cheeks apart and pressed a finger into my thong. My head spun.

She kept kissing me. She sat on a kitchen chair and pointed to her lap. I thought I was going to sit, but she had a different idea.

"Lie across my lap," she said. I hesitated a little. I wasn't entirely sure what was going to happen. She patted her lap. "Come." It was a sexual demand, and I shivered a little.

"No. Why?"

"I'm going to spank you."

"What? Why?" The idea seemed strange to me. I knew that spanking was a sexual thing for some people, but I'd certainly never been spanked.

"You kicked me in the ass. This is payback." I protested that I'd apologized, but she had not accepted it. That never occurred to me. Who wouldn't accept an apology?

"You kicked me because you were angry. That's how you felt at that moment. I don't think you should apologize for showing the truth of how you feel. But you'd better be prepared to deal with the consequences." Getting spanked was the consequence. "I won't be anywhere near as hard as you were," she promised. That just made me feel bad.

I laid across her lap, grateful there were no arms on the chair. She hiked my dress up to my waist. She liked to pull my dress up. She slapped me. It wasn't hard, but it was unexpected and shocking. Then she gently kissed my butt cheek where she'd hit me. I moved to get up, but she kept me down. Slap! This one was a little harder. She rubbed the area and gave it a kiss. When she moved her hand away, I tensed up for another spank, but nothing came.

Slap! She'd fooled me. This slap sent a tingle through me. She rubbed and kissed my ass, but it was more sensual than the last time. I was enjoying the feeling. Slap! Right in the middle, so she got both cheeks.

She bent down to kiss my asshole through my panties. I almost exploded. No one has ever kissed me there. And here she is, kissing me through my underwear. She kissed me twice more, and my panties were soaked. She ran her fingers along the fabric, down the crack of my ass to my pussy. Her fingers rubbed and stroked me. When she slipped her fingers under the elastic and pulled them down, I was a mess. "You're dripping on me. Lick it off."

Her words ripped me out of my revery. I sank to my knees beside the chair and looked at her jeans. There was a wet spot on her thigh. I kissed the spot, tasting myself on her dirty jeans. She grabbed my chin with her hand and I looked up at her. She pushed me back so I sat on my haunches. "Take my jeans off." There were five metal buttons that easily undid. When I opened them up, I could see her pubic hair. She had no underwear on. I pulled them down to her ankles. She put her hand on my head to balance herself as she stepped out of them. Then she pulled my head into her crotch. I kissed and licked her for a few minutes before she stepped away from me. "Up."

I stood up and followed her to the bed. She stopped, arms out, and I reached around to undo her shirt and take it from her body. She stood naked in front of me. I tossed the shirt aside. She turned and circled her finger around. I obediently turned and let her unzip my dress. It fell to the floor. I was in my white bra for only a moment before it was on the floor. She laid back on the bed and patted her lap again.

I straddled her hips. "Play with your tits." I cupped my breasts, stroking and massaging my nipples so they got harder. She grabbed my thighs and told me to pinch my nipples harder. I squirmed a little as I pinched harder. She groaned as I rubbed myself against her mons. "Finger yourself." I moved my hand down my body. When I got to my belly, there was a new order. "Move up. Bring your pussy up to my face so I can watch."

I dragged my pussy along her body, spreading my legs and hovering over her face. I rubbed my clit. "Pull on your lips. Open yourself up." I did as I was told, pulling my lips, entering myself, showing off. I was soaking and my fingers went in and out easily. I curled two fingers inside and worked at my clit with the other hand. I could feel my orgasm building. She reached from behind and inserted a thumb inside me, joining mine. That left her fingers pressed deliciously against my perineum. "Fuck yourself until you come on my face."

Hearing her voice made me shudder. My breath hitched and grew uneven as I moaned and groaned. My entire pussy was on display to her, close up and engorged. My orgasm crested, and I felt come dripping down my fingers and onto her face. She moaned, and I felt her tongue lapping at my hand. Both my clit and G-spot surged, and I quaked and rocked for so long I felt dizzy. I finally withdrew my hands, letting her pull me down onto her face as she savored me. Breathless, I collapsed beside her, spent.

After a few minutes of rest, we started again. All night long she told me what to lick, to move, to squeeze, to offer her, to take from her.

When the morning alarm went off on my phone, I knew I had to leave.

"What are you doing?"

"The bakery. I have to get to work." I put on my bra and panties and grabbed my wrinkled dress from the floor. I am glad I will be wearing an apron over top. As I pulled up the zipper on my dress, I turned and looked at Marti. She looked forlorn. Devastated. "I have to go." She looked sad. "I have a job, you know."

"So do I."

"Mine includes baking bread at 5am. You get to hang out in casinos, get high, and have sex all night long."

"I have such a great job. Stop! Don't move!"

"What? What is it?" I was standing near the window and I looked around, thinking there was some kind of danger around me. I looked at her. She was looking at me. Her hand was between her legs, pleasuring herself.

"Just stand there." Her hand moved faster.

"Marti."

"Shh. Don't. Move." I moved. I walked to the bed, turned around, and hiked up my dress. I bent over and looked back to make sure she had a good look. I slipped my dirty panties off. She was close to an orgasm.

Her legs were wide, and I watched her for a moment. I squeezed her nipple and kissed her. "Enjoy." I pressed my panties onto her face. She moaned as she orgasmed.

Chapter 10

Marti showed up at the bakery hours later, soaking wet from the rain and high as a kite. She had a fresh cut on her lip, but that didn't stop her from smoking. It left blood on the filter. Jean headed to her table with a small glass of water. I thought it was to insist she put the cigarette out, but it was to hold her ashes. Jean had it bad for her. All Marti did was grunt a thank you and settle herself in front of the window. She watched the rain run down the glass.

I joined her at the table, bringing a coffee and a raspberry danish. She looked like she had gotten into a scrap with someone. Her ripped jeans were more ripped. Her jacket was dirtier. There was a stupid smudge of dirt on her cheek that looked like a bad makeup artist was trying to make a blue-eyed beauty look like a scamp.

She rolled her cigarette between her fingers. She told me she tried to quit once. Only once. She ended up in the hospital after taking a cessation drug and smoking, anyway. Nicotine poisoning. She was 15. She was now 34. That was a long time ago. "The rain is so beautiful," she said wistfully. "The glass is a portal between worlds. The city looks stunning because the rain has distorted it. The streaks blend together to make it look beautiful."

How high was she? "Not many people think Falls City is beautiful."

She took a deep drag off her cigarette and looked at me with soft eyes. "In the depths of chaos, beauty finds its life."

"A physicist, a professor, and now a poet?"

"I spent a weekend with one, once. She always spoke in poetry. She tasted like cast iron and cardamom. Thanks for the coffee. And danish. I like your danish."

"I like yours, too." I surprised myself when I said that, since it was clear I wasn't talking about pastry.

"I bought something for you." She reached into her jacket and from nowhere, she pulled out a slender book. A real paper and ink book. The Red Hen's Parish Cook Book: a collection of well tested recipes selected by the Women of the First Congregational Church, Red Hen, Michigan. 1924. "I read some of it. It has a recipe for something called pineapple upside-down cake."

She handed me the dusty 129-year-old cookbook. A faint cloud of dust rose, carrying with it the scent of aged paper and rancid butter. The once vibrant red binding had faded to a muted shade of pink–raspberry?–its edges frayed from years of handling. Traces of flour and oil stains adorn the cover and pages.

Turning the yellowed pages felt amazing. I'd never held a book this old. The texture was rough and uneven. I held it to my nose. How could I not? The faint aroma of spices and herbs seeped from the pages. Scattered throughout the margins are handwritten notes and annotations. Five lines crossed out the recipe from Miss Compton for Mint Sauce (for lamb) with the comment, "No good." Someone marked Mrs. Franklin Paidar's recipe for Velvet Sponge Cake with a penciled X. A time when women took the husband's first and last name, giving their identities up for him.

A handwritten note on killing and plucking a chicken was tucked into the poultry section. Plunge the dead bird into boiling water to make it easier to remove the feathers, though a dry-plucked bird has superior favor. Good to know, should I begin killing and plucking chickens. I'm a baker, not a butcher.

There is a stereotype for bakers. We are female, or at least feminine. We are detail oriented. If you leave out a vital ingredient too many times, you are no longer a baker, but a failure with an expensive habit of wasting food. We are generally realistic individuals. The profit margins on handmade baked goods at a privately owned store are shockingly low. We have to understand the science of substitution when ingredients are unavailable. And we like to work with our hands. There are exceptions, of course, and many bakers do not conform to these stereotypes. But I do.

The constant challenge of unobtainable or poor quality ingredients these days is quite remarkable. I will try to order Hennerman's Fine Unbleached Flour for my cake and find it's not expected back on the market for six months.

Do I substitute a different flour and change my cakes for six months? Or do I go with a new flour altogether and eschew the old, point forward? It matters to customers. They may not understand why something tastes different today than yesterday, they only know that it does. And oddly, they won't tell you they've noticed the difference, or ask as to why there is a difference. Instead, they just stop showing up. 'I don't like the taste of this tartlet anymore. I'm never coming back.'

It's not that there are a lot of other bakeries to go to, but there are a lot of places to buy prepackaged, industrial pastries. I doubt there is a single store that sells food that doesn't sell some kind of weirdly textured, overly sweet roll in a crinkly plastic wrap. Except bakeries.

And those customers, the ones who don't like the change from Hennerman's flour to Diony's flour and don't tell you, will tell everyone else. You, unfortunately, will be the last to find out, and always on social media. It's mostly harmless. Except when there's been some grave misunderstanding and the person who asked for strawberry tarts actually wanted field berry tarts and they say it's your fault and wage a war online against you and your business goes up in smoke because they have insane followers who do things like bomb stores. Except them.

And I would like to say it's rare that stores are fire-bombed. But if it were rare, I probably wouldn't have even considered writing about it. It is common. The bombings, I mean. Not the misunderstandings. Well, those too. In fact, I sometimes wonder if they are just performative complaints in an effort to stir the masses. Go viral with your hate, and some unknown person with a grudge and a desire for fame will embrace that hate and channel it for you.

The queer bookstore on Madison was fire-bombed two years ago, and the resulting fire took out a clothing store and a deli. The Japanese food place over on 45th had a Molotov cocktail thrown through the window five years ago and half a city block went up in flames. Three died. I don't think Marti worked on that, despite being in Homicide. The federal government handled it. They found the guy who threw the bomb. He didn't like the wasabi in his Unagi Chazuke.

Selling baked goods requires consistency because we must deal with your anemoia, that yearning for a past you never experienced. Who doesn't want grandma's warm apple pie or great aunty's blueberry strudel with a drizzle of lemon icing? The crisp layers of a good strudel will crumble under your bite, stick to your lips as you pull your mouth from the pastry. You are then faced with the exquisitely painful decision of chewing the sweetness already in your mouth and risking small pieces of flakey crust falling to the table, or licking your lips and getting blueberry on them. In the end, regardless of what you choose, you lick your finger and tap at the flakes to pick them up, and slowly, reverently, put the wayward delight in your mouth. But she never baked that for you. Ever. You want what you never had.

A cloud of smoke in my face drew me out of the book. Marti was looking at me, one eyebrow cocked and a smirk on her face. "Do you like it?"

"I am not a cookbook collector," I said, flipping through the pages. "But some of this is amazing! Beautiful photographs for the time. Look at this apple pie." Even though the image was washed out, you could see the glimmer of the egg wash on the perfectly browned crust. I read the ingredient list. "Of course. One egg white and whole milk. So shiny."

I looked through the book a bit more while she smoked, but I found myself watching her lips. She would bring the cigarette up to her mouth and part her lips slightly before slipping the filter in. Her lips would close around the butt and she would suck in, making the ember glow with life. Her lips would separate very faintly and she would pull it out. If her lips were dry, they would be plucked by the cigarette paper and snap back. Then she would hold her breath and lick her lips, her tongue barely flickering out and in. Then and only them would she close her lips again and exhale through her nose.

"What happened to your lip?"

She instinctively touched her tongue to the cut. "Would you believe me if I told you I got high and fell face first into a wall?"

"No." I believe she could get stoned and fall face first into a wall. I just don't believe that's what caused this injury.

"I got into a fight."

"That I believe. Why?"

"Some big guy was harassing some little guy. I don't know his name, but I've seen the little guy around. Harmless. The big guy had him by the shoulder, knocked some cans out of his hands–you know, empties he was collecting–and shook his finger in his face. Threatening him. I guess he was shaking the little guy down for money, but for this little guy, those cans were his money. Fifty cents each at the recycling depot. I just thought, what the fuck? I said, 'Dude, you can't get blood from a stone.' Big guy was too stupid to understand what I meant. He starts shaking the little guy, so I knocked his hand off the little guy's shoulder. He took a swing and hit me. I took a swing and hit him. Like that."

"Was that the end of it?"

"No. He took another swing. Broke two of my ribs."

"Just two? What did you do?"

"Shot him. Just a little bit. In the hand. Very fixable."

"Oh my–You what? Have you been to the hospital?"

"Not yet."

"Why not?"

"I'd just shot a guy, so I had to get out of there before the cops showed up. I headed down the street, but I was moving slowly on account of my ribs. When I heard the sirens, I ducked into a store. It was a bookstore. Like an actual bookstore! And, voila!" She held out her hands toward the book.

I was astonished. She was protecting a stranger, got beat up, shot someone and found a 129-year-old cookbook for me. I found out over time she often felt the need to help the underdog, and at times, did so very foolishly.

"Are you going to the hospital?"

"I'll go to a walk-in a little later."

"Will you get in trouble? Can they track you down?" Instead of being concerned that she shot someone 'just a little bit,' I was concerned she would get caught.

"Nah. I know the beat cops in the area. Davidson and Driver. Assholes, but they're lazy. Too lazy to pursue this kind of thing."

"A shooting?"

"But just a little bit of a shooting. The guy's probably already been to a walk-in, paid his money, got his hand fixed like new. No harm, no foul."

My concern gave way to shock when I realized she actually shot a man and wasn't going to face any consequences. "But Marti, you shot a man."

"A bad man. Just a little bit. In defense of a smaller man. That's not illegal. If I bring the cops in, the big guy is the one who would get arrested. Why would I do that to him? He just got shot. I'm giving him a break when you think about it."

The Immediate-Threat Defense law allows you to use a proportional reaction to an immediate threat. He hit her twice, so she shot him a little. She's right. She committed no crime, but he had. I've never known anyone else, not before and not since Marti, who has ever shot anyone for any reason, however minor the resulting wound.

"Do you want me to take you to the hospital?"

"No."

"What can I do for you?"

"Kiss me before I go."

"To the hospital?" I asked as I leaned across the table.

"Come over here. I can't lean over."

I stood up and walked around the table to kiss her. I avoided the cut on her lip when I kissed her. She put her hand on my back to pull me closer, hold me longer. "You'll go to the hospital?"

"Walk me to my car." She got up and winced. I put my hand against her side and she winced again. "Oww. Do you like hurting me?"

"No! Sorry. Of course not!" I just happened to be a natural at it. As we walked out, she asked me to read over the cookbook and choose a recipe to make for her. She said she did not mind whether it was a dessert or a main, just something I thought she'd like. She complained she'd not had a home cooked meal in years, and couldn't think of anyone better than me to give her the pleasure. Marti could make it feel like a privilege to do something for her.

I opened the umbrella, but she preferred to pull up her hoodie and walk in the rain. Her car was half a block away. The world was almost silent. I heard only the sounds of wind and rain. She thrived in the rain in a way I never understood.

We got to her car, and she leaned against it, pulling me close to her. "You're making me wet," I told her.

"Don't I know it."

"I mean, from the rain. You're negating my use of the umbrella by getting me wet because you're soaked."

"I am soaked." She bent to kiss me. The rain thrummed on my umbrella, a police siren sounded in the distance and the sounds of car tires splashing through puddles filled the air. It was magical.

"Do you trust me?"

"Not in the slightest."

"Ha! That's a really good answer. You probably shouldn't. But I would be remiss, dear lady, if I didn't warn you."

"Warn me? Now I'm really suspicious."

"Not suspicious enough. Do yourself a favor. Go to First National Bank, in person, just you. Remove all other signatories from every account you have. Both personal and business. Include your credit accounts. Then get a 30-day credit block, so they have to speak to you in person before giving you a line of credit."

I shook my head. "A quantum physicist, an English professor, a poet, and now a financial advisor. Why would I do that? It will hobble the business."

It was her turn to shake her head. "I can't tell you that."

"I can ask my accountant what she–"

"No. Don't tell Tiffany. Tell no one, except at the bank. Not even after it's done. If anyone asks, tell them you are surprised and will get that fixed as soon as you can. Stall for the 30 days."

"No."

"Yes."

"No."

"I really like you."

"I really like you too."

"Don't say I didn't warn you." She kissed me again and pushed me away, then got into her car. I stood in the rain as she drove away. The rain wasn't magical anymore. It was cold, and I felt like I was drowning. Why the warning?

I've worked with Tiffany O'Brien for about four years. She's a partner at Gallagher and O'Brien, and I trust her implicitly. Marti, on the other hand, was an addict, and the only thing I could trust about her was her unreliability and her constant desire for sex and drugs and booze. She was late for everything, sometimes disappeared for weeks on end, and was always getting into fights.

It was also true, I eventually admitted, that she had helped me in ways I never understood. And until now, I never questioned. I never asked her how she managed to have city employees to repair my bakery back in 2049. But it was done the next day at no cost to me. In fact, I made a small profit. I never asked how she stopped that man from ruining the 2-day-old food I left outside the shop for people who were hungry. But she stopped it for me, and I kicked her in return.

As I walked into the bakery, the most important questions hit me. How did she know Tiffany was my accountant? And my bank was First National? I stood in the doorway thinking about this until a customer pushed past me to get in. It's because she's a private investigator.

I went into the office, grabbed a bunch of documents from the safe, and told Grace and Jean I was heading to the bank. It took half an hour to go through all of their paperwork, prove who I was and, most importantly, that I alone owned the bakery and the building. I removed Tiffany as the signatory and discovered that Quincy Gallagher was also a signatory on a one million dollar line of credit I didn't know I had. There was just $1,000 owing on the line, though two months previously it had been $900,000. It seemed that Tiffany and Quincy were using a line of credit under my name, but paying it off. I closed the line, blocked my credit for 30 days, and left the bank with a weird feeling in my stomach.

Have you ever done something for yourself, but aren't entirely sure why you did it? Like some angel whispered in your ear, 'Don't get on that flight' or 'Go to that movie starring the actor you hate.' And it turns out the flight crashes and everyone dies, or your house burns down, but you're okay because you were at the movies?

That's how I felt.

Chapter 11

I saw Marti three weeks later. We were at my apartment:
I don't like the neighborhood she lives in. And I had
promised to cook from the Red Hen cookbook.

Choosing a recipe that would be tolerable by today's
standards was the hardest part. The stuffed pork tender-
loin with bananas sounded unappetizing. If I served her
stewed tripe and celery, she would leave me (and justifiably
so). I settled on curried beef with vinegar and grape jelly
on the side. We both agreed the beef did not require the
vinegar or the jelly.

After we ate, and she ate so little, she stuck her head out
the window and took a hit of Shadow. I was disappointed.

"Do you really need to get high?"

"Yep."

"Why?"

"Because the food was good and now it's over, but I still
want the good feeling."

"There are other good things we can do."

She was high, of course, and very gentle. It's like every-thing was in slow motion: she kissed me slowly, her lips lingering on mine. She touched me slowly, her fingers trailing down my arm and over my fingers. Shadow only lasts about 20 minutes so we were still in early foreplay when she sobered up.

She sat partially up in bed. "Come here." I sat on her hips, and she raised her knees up so I could lean back on them. She liked the word 'come' because it was so innocent and so dirty. 'Come here' could mean 'please join me,' or it could mean 'I will bring you to orgasm.' Since we were both nude, it meant the latter.

She put one hand on my neck and pulled me to her lips, kissing me and running her fingers through my hair. She French kissed me, her tongue thick and full in my mouth. She bent her head and raised my breast to her lips. Her fingers played with the nipple on my other breast until she switched. "I can feel your wet pussy on my stomach," she said. If it wasn't true when she said it, it was true now.

She shifted her upper body flat on the bed, bringing me with her. She kept her knees bent and spread them wider. It gave her hands access to me from behind. She kept kissing me as she worked both hands. One hand entered my pussy while the other pulled on my lips and clit. It felt otherworldly. The harder she kissed, the further she entered me. I kept myself angled just right for her, for my pleasure.

I shook a little and pressed myself down against her body to get steady again. She was slick, whether from sweat, from me, or both. My pussy felt hot and wild and I pressed back to force her in deeper. My mind went blank as she pressed against my G-spot and rubbed my clit, and I moaned as I orgasmed. She moaned as I orgasmed, enjoying it almost as much as I did. "On my face, now. Let me taste your come," she said as I began to relax my body. I eagerly moved up her body and offered my pussy to her luscious lips. Her expert tongue began to lick and probe. She held my hips and moved me forward so her mouth had a path to more flesh.

"Turn around, fuck me." I turned but sat on her face and leaned forward. I balanced on one hand and used the other to play with her pussy. It was getting difficult to think. I felt another orgasm growing as she raised her hips up for me. I laid against her, both hands and my tongue buried in her pussy as she continued eating me. As I orgasmed again, I pressed my tongue hard against her clit and slipped my fingers in and out of her. Beneath me, her body trembled, and we orgasmed together. Hers went on longer and I could feel her hot breath in my wetness. As it subsided, I rolled off her, panting to catch my breath. She rested her hand on the crack of my ass as she brought her breathing under control.

Not knowing when you're finally finished having sex is both a blessing and a curse for lesbians. With Marti, you stop when you're about to pass out from pleasurable exhaustion.

I showered in the morning by myself, despite Marti's playful request to join me. I came out to find her sitting naked by the window, a sliver of morning sun shining on her body. Smoke curled around her face like a veil. She is lean, her jaw is strong, her lips full. Her arms and legs are sinewy. She is pale, but almost everyone in Falls City is. We don't see a lot of sun. Her breasts are small and, I think, her nipples are almost always hard. She has a lot of scars: some are red and angry, others are whiter than white, and a few are raised and rough. She flicked the ashes from her cigarette out the window and caught sight of my reflection in the glass. She has a beautiful smile.

"Can you tell me how you knew about Tiffany and Quincy? And the loan?"

"I can, high level, I guess. I was looking into some strange loans for a client and traced it to Gallagher and O'Brien. I saw you were on their client list."

"I don't understand what they were doing, though."

"To put it simply, they would take out loans using legit businesses, then repay those loans with dirty money. Drug money, mostly. That's why you had a million dollar loan you didn't know about."

"How long did you know?"

"A couple of months. I had to let them repay it or you'd have been on the hook for the million."

I admit I got a little salty about Marti not telling me earlier, as if somehow she was responsible for putting me in financial danger. It didn't help that she did not go to the police, either. She said she no longer had a good relationship with them, which is fair enough, but what about all the innocent businesses like me that could have suffered?

"I can't save everyone."

"Why me?"

"You're worth saving."

I used to have a recurring dream of trying to get to my university lecture using the stairs. Sometimes the stairs would lead to a brick wall, other times to dank, never-ending basement hallways. The stairs I need are in sight, but I couldn't get there. I'm running faster and I end up in a movie theater. I think I know the way, and I end up in the library. I am close. I am across campus in a bowling alley. There are stairs leading here and there, but never to my lecture. My mind is racing, my body is racing. I am frantic. I will be late. The stairs lead nowhere. Escher would be proud of my nightmare.

This dream of constant effort and failure captured the essence of my sense of worth. My lack of worth. I will never succeed at the simplest of tasks and no one will help. I am fated to go everywhere but get nowhere. My failure is preordained. I am always alone.

We all have moments when we feel inadequate. It's like I was trapped in a dream of failure and unworthiness, unable to break free.

I felt that for a long time in my life. Even when I bought the bakery, I felt like a failure. I bought it through the misery of others. The world was a mere backdrop to my struggle to succeed. When Marti came smashing through the bakery door, part of me was relieved. I thought that was the end of my shop and I didn't have to risk becoming successful. My shop had since become popular, but I felt like I hadn't earned it, that the success was undeserved. As I watched her smash chairs and windows and tables, I thought, "Ah ha! I knew this would end up failing."

When the place was repaired so quickly, I was absolutely thrown. It was like I was being forced to keep the shop. I was forced to honor the effort others put in to repair my shop. I was being forced to succeed. I was forced to become popular for a few minutes. I worked harder to handle the influx of customers. I hired staff and wasn't working alone 15 hours a day. I could take a day off. I could pay off my mortgage and start to put money aside to give to Li and Zhao if I see them again.

It wasn't an instant fix. It's hard to trust that we're loved and accepted by others when we don't think we are worth something. I lived with a constant undercurrent of expecting less because I felt like less.

Until that morning, when Marti firmly said I was worth saving. It seemed so factual, so honest. When this naked woman sitting, smoking, in the morning sun said I was worth saving, I believed her.

Tiffany and Quincy were later arrested for money laundering, and mine was one of many innocent businesses caught in the middle. The police wanted me to come to the station for an interview. Marti had some thoughts on that.

"Tell them you want to meet somewhere neutral, a café or something. Bring your lawyer."

"I don't have a lawyer."

"Find one who specializes in helping victims of fraud. When the police ask you why you brought a lawyer, tell them it's because you don't really know what's going on and you need advice."

"I don't understand what happened and I do need advice."

"See? Lawyer. Even someone who has criminal law experience."

She was adamant that you should always have a lawyer with you when questioned by Falls City Police. She said detectives spend 10 hours a day, day in and day out, interviewing people. Over the years, they become experts. Whereas I have never been interviewed by a detective in my life.

I followed her advice. When we met, one of the detectives got upset. "Why do you need a lawyer? Have you done something wrong?" My lawyer shot that down quickly. He told me later if I had answered 'no, I haven't done anything,' the detective would find something, speeding, jaywalking, violating some law from 1865, and arrest me for lying to the police. The charge would get thrown out, but until then, I would be in police custody and more willing to talk to them in order to get out. Under that pressure, I say might something that can be misinterpreted against me. It's all quite frightening.

I had told Sandy all about it before attending the interview, and she asked if she could come along. "I want to be your Plus One. Do they have that? A friend that can come along?" They did not. But she relished in every detail, in the thrill of it all.

Chapter 12

Later that month, I headed to Cliffport for the Hennerman Baking Championships, an invitation-only competition for small bakeries like mine. Because it is for small bakeries, only one baker can attend. It has been quite a while since I'd worked alone, but I was confident. I knew some of the others bakers. Malcolm Gladstone, a baker from Slayerton, would be there. We'd met at previous competitions, and his sense of humor saved me a few times from smacking a judge or two. The unusual thing about him was that he was legally blind. He lost his sight during a solar eclipse by, in his words, "being stupid enough to think my eyes were stronger than the sun." He wore dark sunglasses now, not only to protect what little sight he had, but to stop people from running and screaming from him. It looks like a small universe in his eyes.

Shirley Summers was another baker I knew. She came from Little Cove on the Atlantic side of the country. She was cool, in a New England sort of way. As nice as can be, until it was competition time. As soon as the clock started, she became a monster, and was not above sabotaging anyone she thought might beat her. Since there were 2,000 starting bakers, there were a lot of dirty deeds to be done.

When I flew from Falls City to Cliffport, we had to fly over a large swath of what was left of Texas. They'd picked a fight with China and the entire country paid the price. Texas, New Mexico and Utah were wastelands. I have no great desire to see them from the air. Or the ground. More than 19 million Americans died during the three days of war. There just wouldn't be much left to see. I feigned sleep.

Cliffport is stunning. The seaside city offers breathtaking views of the ocean stretching out endlessly to the horizon. It is mercifully dry, sometimes going days without rain. The fires weren't so bad this past year, and the air was clean and fresh. The town itself is a blend of quasi-cottages, expensive hotels, upscale boutiques, and bustling restaurants, all perched precariously on the edge of the cliff. They used to be more than 100 yards away, but erosion was bringing the sea closer. Narrow winding streets lead down to the rocky beach below. One stumble and I think you're either dead on the rocks or lost in the sea. But that could just be me.

I planned my dishes for all three days. The Raspberry Danish Delights on day one, Blueberry Whimsy Puffs on two and the Lavender Bliss Cookies as the finale on day three. The last day was always the shortest in the kitchen, so cookies were a safe bet. During the day, it was all about the contest. No one was friends with anyone. But after you submitted your entry–we were judged each day, but the standings weren't revealed until the last day–you were free to do as you please. Some bakers hung around, watching the competition. Others took in the beautiful scenery. I was one of those who spent my time outdoors.

The sun is mesmerizing when you don't see it often. The sunrise bathes the city in golden light as the sun peeks over the horizon, casting a warm glow across the landscape. In the evenings, the sky erupts into a symphony of colors as the sun sets behind the ocean, painting the cliffs in hues of orange, pink, and purple. I didn't see grey once while I was there.

My friends and I sat on the beach after the first day's bake, wondering if Marti had ever seen a setting sun like this. I decided to call and leave a dirty message, just to make her feel jealous. I asked my friends what they thought of the views, looking for inspiration. I told them I wanted to describe the landscape to someone, but needed to make it "more." Shirley said I should lie a little, describe what isn't there, let my imagination run free. Malcolm laughed and said he couldn't see the damned landscape, but he liked the smell of the ocean. Perfect.

I walked away from my friends–I'm far too discreet to let anyone hear what I was going to say–and called Marti and left her a message: "The sun is going down and I'm hot. Sweat is dripping down and I can't stop it. In front of me is the ocean, spraying herself all over my face. It's salty when I lick my lips. I'm thinking of you. Call me tonight. Ten o'clock. I want to make love to you with my voice."

That evening I am prepared. Freshly showered, lying in bed naked under the covers, holding my phone and staring at the clock. Ten o'clock comes and goes, but there is no phone call. By 10:15pm, I start to worry that she isn't going to call at all. There is no way for me to check that she received my message. At 10:30pm, I decided to call her. No answer.

I wondered what it was that she was up to, and decided I really did not want to know. Instead, I thought, what would she do? If she were lying in bed waiting for a lover to call, what would she do? I swear it was like she was whispering in my ear. I began to touch myself, recalling her expert touch and trying to replicate it. I ran my fingers in circles and up and down.

It took a little longer than usual to arouse myself fully because, just as I would let my mind enjoy the pleasure, it would snap back into what I had planned for my next step. Finally, after quite a bit of pleasurable coaxing, I could feel my orgasm rising in me. I dialed my phone.

"Marti, it's Billie...I, uh, I am thinking of you. Thinking of your lips and...hands and tongue and your kisses and touches. You feel so good inside me." I could barely choke out the words as my body began to spasm in ecstasy.

Thinking of her while saying those words was powerful. I finally just dropped the phone on my bed beside me and let the orgasm roll over me. I moaned, maybe a little louder than normal, as I came. I wanted her to be part of this, to listen to the message and become aroused herself.

I stopped after just one orgasm and turned on my side, breathing heavily into the phone. I whispered, "I'm going to lick my fingers," and proceeded to noisily suck and lick as promised. I dried my fingers on the sheets and rolled onto my back, ready to fall asleep. I looked at the phone. It had already disconnected. I hoped she would get an earful.

Chapter 13

When I flew back, I had made plans for Marti to pick me up from the airport. I was shocked when instead, a young blonde woman–not much more than a girl–was there holding a placard with my name on it.

"Hi Billie? I'm Lori. Lori Harring. I'm Marti's secretary. She asked me to pick you up."

"Why can't she be here herself?"

"She got herself into a bit of a jam the other night. Nothing serious, but she's being held in jail! I can't believe it. Trespassing. She called the office and asked me to come get you."

Lori was a young university graduate, and she had somehow stumbled upon Marti's secretarial job call. She thought it sounded exciting. I found out more about her on the drive to the jail. We were going to bail Marti out. Lori's father is a police officer in another town, her mother a teacher or something. I couldn't follow everything she was saying. I was jetlagged, and she was a fast and constant talker. It's like the very idea of breathing was exciting to her and she just had to talk about it.

Lori very kindly told me all about the Falls City landmarks we were passing, as if I was a tourist. Of course, she was the tourist. "That building there is the first office of Mayor Hadleberg back in 1806," she said. "I studied Falls City once I got the job. Over there is the Dalhousie Arms. That's where Ian Graham overdosed. Do you know his music? He had such a great voice, so sorrowful. Would you like to stop for coffee? A little pick-me-up after your long flight?" She has a cheeriness that belongs in Cliffport, not Falls City. I'm sure either the city or Marti will ruin that for her soon enough, but I wasn't going to contribute to it.

"I'd love coffee, yes. How sweet of you."

"Oh, ha ha! No problem. There's a Big Bean, we can stop there."

"Have you been to the jail before?"

"No. First time. What about you?"

"Never. Do you know how to bail someone out?"

"Not really. I know you have to pay some money. I have access to the business accounts, so no problem."

Marti gave this kid access to hundreds of thousands of dollars after just a couple of days. I no longer felt bad about trusting Tiffany, an actual certified accountant, with my money.

We ordered coffees at Big Bean, and she happily paid. "All on the company dime," she said. What a strange turn of phrase for such a young woman.

"I like your car," I said as we got back inside to continue our journey.

"Oh, it's a company car Marti bought for me. She's so nice."

"Sure is. How long have you been working for her?"

"Almost two weeks now. She's, uh, pretty amazing. I mean, as a detective."

"Private investigator."

"Yes, right. Here we are."

We parked at the jail—a $25 flat fee—and walked through the glass doors into the reception area. Payments could be made at the third window. I sat while Lori did her thing. I felt like I was invading on company time. Lori returned to my side, happy to have paid. "Just $40,000. I guess that's good, right?"

"Are you sure it was just trespassing?" She searched the paperwork and said it was trespassing with criminal intent.

"Hello gorgeous," Marti said as she walked into the lobby.

"Hi!" Lori's cheery voice ran out.

"Hi Lori, thanks for coming to get me." She slipped her arm around my waist and gave me a deep kiss. I gave a quick glance over at Lori. She watched us with a wistful adoration. I gave Marti a squeeze around her waist and could feel her wince. She gave me a look, and I stayed silent. Once we were outside, Marti asked she be taken to an AutoMedi. We got into the car–Lori in the front seat and she and I in the back–and Marti showed me her wound. Someone had stabbed her in the side with a pen. I asked her if she reported it to the authorities. She laughed.

"It was a guard that stabbed me." She said she had arrested the woman's husband for killing his mistress. The guard blamed Marti. I was genuinely shocked. "Why blame you?" I asked. She said the family and friends of some murderers don't want such a public eye turned on such a personal failing. They cannot believe they loved and trusted someone who could be a monster, and they take it out on everyone else. "All I know it's, it hurts almost as much as getting shot."

In the midst of it all, she asked how I fared in the competition. I told her I was in the top 20, my best showing ever. The competition had been stiff, and I was certain Shirley had put something foul in my danish.

We arrived quickly at an AutoMedi, Lori following Marti's directions. She knew the way quite well, which both concerned and did not surprise me. "Stay here. Give me 15 minutes," Marti said as she got out of the car. It took her just 12 to return. She said she was good as new.

Lori drove us to the office while we made out in the back seat. I felt a little self-conscious, and Marti kept all her actions above the neckline. Once we were at the office,

Marti and I transferred to her car, and Lori went back to work.

"That girl has a thing for you."

"No way. I just hired her."

"Do you think she took the job because you're so sexy?"

"Well now, I am sexy. But I think she took the job because it's interesting and it pays well. Besides, I told her right up front I wasn't going to fuck her. No fucking the secretary."

"Did you really say that?"

"Yes. I wanted to be really clear. That thing with Susan kind of ruined everything, you know? So I said no to fucking, yes I use drugs. I'm going to fuck things up, and hell yeah, this is going to be the best job of your life." I wished she gave me that kind of warning when we first started to see each other. But like Lori, it wouldn't have stopped me.

Once we were firmly ensconced in my home, I felt like I could breathe. I was upset that Marti had expected me to traipse all over Falls City with her secretary when she could have just as easily sent word that I would have to find my own way home. I told her so, but all she did was kiss me and squeeze my breast. "I'm glad you're back."

"Did you get my messages?"

"'The ocean is spraying herself all over my face.' Great line. I couldn't call back. I was busted a couple of hours later."

"What about my other message?" Marti hadn't listened to the message I'd left while I was orgasming. I didn't tell her what it was, but I told her to listen to her messages while I showered. Within a few minutes, she walked into the bathroom naked and got into the shower with me. She hadn't showered in a couple of days and wanted to get clean before getting dirty with me.

"The message was great, but it cut off. It only takes a two-minute message. I didn't get to hear you finish coming. Only the start."

"You can listen live, if you'd like."

She turned me around and wrapped her arms around me, pressing into my back, the water hitting her back. "You are magnificent," she said as she played with my nipples. "You turn me on when I see you, hear you. I'm keeping your orgasm and I want you to send more. I love to hear you moan, to hear your breathing."

I had never left any message like that, never so raw, honest. Thinking she was going to keep it excited me. Her hands excited me. The water dripping down her face onto my shoulders excited me. I reached back and grabbed her muscular ass, and it excited me. We got dirty before we got clean.

I knew Marti's life was complicated, far too complex for me to become deeply involved. The next morning, as she again sat naked by the window smoking, she said she appreciated that. "Too many women want parts of me they can't have. I don't lie about who I am. You're just one of the few who had believed me when I say I'm an asshole and you should keep your guard up. That means a lot to me."

She flipped her cigarette out the window and grabbed her inhaler. She became quite used to getting high in front of me, and sometimes I didn't mind. Her body and her words and her thoughts become soft. Like her fury disappears. I interrupted her inhalation and straddled her lap. To take her mind off the drug, at least for a moment, I kissed and caressed her. I pinched her erect nipples and slipped off her lap, between her legs. She put her hand on my head as I ate her. "Fuck, yes! Stick it inside me." She leaned her torso backwards, thrusting her hips forward to give me better access to her pussy. I knew her taste well. She came, gasping and moaning my name. I kissed her, washed up, and headed to work.

Chapter 14

It was early fall when my friend Sandy declared that we must fulfill our childhood dream of going to Paris. Sandy and I weren't friends in childhood. We met as adults. But in our conversations, we realized we both wanted to visit Paris as children. I had never been anywhere in Europe. I had been madly curious about Sainte-Claire-sur-Seine, located just outside Paris. Grace told me she had been to Paris, and it was not all of was cracked up to be. She said I had a good chance of being kidnapped. Jean agreed, but Malcolm thought I'd be fine if I didn't tell anyone I was from America. He recommended driving to Canada and flying from there. Sandy agreed to spend a day and night of our trip in Sainte-Claire-sur-Seine.

Marti had no aversion to me disappearing for two weeks. She pointed out she disappeared all the time without consulting me. She didn't understand why I was asking her if I could go.

"I'm not asking you for permission. I'm letting you know so you didn't get worried when you can't find me."

"So you aren't telling Grace and Jean?"

"Of course I am."

"Then they'd have told me if I asked." If I asked. She could irritate me with her cavalier comments. I didn't consult with her again before I left. I was disappointed she hadn't called or followed up. I know expecting her to miss me was asking too much, but the least she could do was pretend.

Sandy and I drove first to Canada, agreeing that Malcolm's advice was good. A flight from America might be a target for terrorists. A flight from Canada would be ignored. We spent an afternoon and evening in Toronto. It was a beautiful city, with clean air and clean water. People were friendly and everyone spoke English. I thought they spoke French up here. Sandy was fluent in French, so I was going to have to rely on her as a translator no matter where we went. The architecture in Toronto is contemporary boring. Glass buildings mixed with reinforced plasprint boxes. Nothing seemed to be very old or interesting. Sandy and I enjoyed a dinner of locally caught fish. The waiter brought a food-friendly mercury detector to show the levels were acceptable. I wasn't sure if the device was real or performative, but one serving of fish wouldn't kill me. Not right away. We flew out at midnight.

We landed in Paris a few hours later. No protests, no crowd to boo as you got off the plane. Acting Canadian was a smart move.

Paris is stunning. They have old buildings, cobblestone on some of the roads, and an openness that lets you see the sky. In Falls City, everything is close and tall and the buildings block out the sun. Here I feel transported to another world. People are speaking a language I don't understand. I can only guess at the shop signs, and it's freeing. I saw it only through the window of a taxi as we drove to Sainte-Claire-sur-Seine. We were starting our vacation there.

Nestled in the picturesque countryside of northern France, Sainte-Claire-sur-Seine is a well-kept secret for everyone but the most dedicated pastry connoisseur. There are 10,000 people in the town, and four bakeries. Each bakery had their own cafes, both inside and outside. We had booked a room above La Boulangerie des Rêves, the bakery specializing in La Lune de Nuit, The Night Moon. We checked in and headed downstairs for a taste of this celestial pastry. It is exquisite. It is a light choux pastry shell filled with a rich chocolate ganache infused with hints of espresso and cognac. Encased in a glossy chocolate glaze, each bite offers love in a decadent combination of velvety chocolate and warming spirits. I want to send a photograph of this party melting in my mouth to Marti, to make her jealous. La Boulangerie des Rêves does not allow photographs. In the end, I am alright with keeping this to myself. Sandy could not understand my passionate response. She is a heathen.

We walked to the heart of Sainte-Claire-sur-Seine's historic center, where the imposing silhouette of the Church of Saint Pierre dominates the skyline. Built in the 12th century, this architectural masterpiece boasts stunning Gothic architecture and houses an impressive collection of religious artifacts and artwork. No Falls City brutalism here.

We wandered through the winding streets, passing centuries-old timber-framed houses and a bustling market brimming with local delicacies. Sandy agreed to a few sweets from the marketplace, but I was saving myself for Douceur de France Bakery and their Le Jardin Enchanté.

Le Jardin Enchanté is a whimsical pastry that transports you to a magical garden blooming with flavors. It combines layers of flaky puff pastry filled with a luscious raspberry compote and creamy almond frangipane. Topped with a dusting of powdered sugar, it offers a symphony of fruity sweetness and nutty undertones, evoking the vibrant colors and fragrant scents of a French garden in full bloom. As I eat it, telling Sandy my thoughts, I think of how Marti describes the taste of women. I think of her taste: subtly smoky, tangy, and savory, with a hint of Macadamia nut. It's so accurate, I message her my description.

She responded immediately, "Gimme a sec, I gotta try." She didn't follow up. She must have kept herself busy.

For lunch, we selected a bistro that served coq au vin. I complimented my meal with a glass of Villa Pierre wine, sourced from a nearby vineyard. I sent a photograph of the bistro patio to Marti with the message, "No rain." She responded with, "Are you wet anyway?" I blushed and Sandy noticed.

"What'd you get?"

"Coq au vin."

"Smart ass. What was the message?"

I had mentioned Marti long ago, when she was nothing more than a one-night stand. "Remember that woman I told you about?"

"Sure. You don't date very often Billie, it's pretty easy to keep track of every woman you're interested in. What did she send you?"

"She was asking about the weather."

I just wasn't ready to share her. At the next bakery we went to, Le Pain Doré, I chose Le Soleil Levant, a decadent treat of a buttery brioche base infused with tangy notes of pink pepper and adorned with a delicate drizzle of dark chocolate icing. Stunning.

We headed back to the room to pack. We would take a taxi back to Paris for the rest of the vacation. We arrived at our hotel after dark. It was on the third floor of a walk-up, but a concierge carried our bags up. He told us–Sandy, technically–that there has been a terrorist attack at the Place de la Concorde and it was currently off limits, but the western portion of Champs-Élysées was open to pedestrians. Radicals had set off a small bomb, damaging one storefront and a portion of the road.

At Arc de Triomphe, I took a selfie and sent it to Marti with the message: "Victory is mine." I heard nothing from her until we were sitting at an outdoor bistro. When my phone buzzed, Sandy grabbed it. I didn't care, it had a biolock.

"Is she asking about the weather again?"

"How would I know? You have my phone."

"If you're sexting, I need to know."

"Why?"

"Look, Billie, I love Kevin. He's a great husband and a fantastic dad. But..." She leaned close and whispered conspiratorially, "he is a terrible lover."

I laughed. "He can't be that bad. You have three kids!"

"I don't know how we managed that. He once did it to the crease between my thigh and vag. He has no idea, and he won't listen. He thinks grabbing a quicky while the kids are asleep is romantic. I asked him once if we could have music on and he said it would distract him."

Now I laughed really hard and apologized to Sandy for laughing at her. But I couldn't stop. "I am more adventurous than that."

"Let me in on your romantic texts. C'mon, please? Give a girl a break."

"Look, she's unpredictable. I have no idea what she is going to send me. You might be shocked."

"I have a husband who thinks lighting candles is kinky. I want to be shocked." I relented and opened my phone. Sandy leaned over my shoulder so she could see the message. "Thinking of you," accompanied by a photo of her chest in a black shirt. Her nipples were hard.

Sandy squealed in delight. "Oh, my God! That's so sexy. If I sent something like that to Kevin, he'd ask me if it was a new shirt. Can I see what you've sent her?" She was disappointed by the 'Victory' photo and with my "No rain" message, but liked the "Are you wet anyway?" response.

We were able to get to the Eiffel Tower, but the lineup to go up the elevator was an estimated two hours. We opted instead to sit on the grass with a bottle of wine and some bread and cheese we'd bought at a nearby market. I told her about Marti. Not everything. She wasn't interested in everything. She wanted to know about the sex.

"Is it good?"

"It's great."

"You don't have a lot of experience to compare, though."

"One time when she was...using her mouth, I bucked my hips so hard she bit her tongue. Neither of us knew until she came up for air and she had blood on her lips!"

"Oh, my God! Vampire lover! Show me her picture."

"I don't have one."

"Bullshit. You have her nipples! Don't you have her face?"

I didn't. I had a dark, blurry photo of the two of us, and no amount of autocorrect would fix it. Sandy asked me to ask Marti to send a photograph of her lips. I laughed and said there would be no telling what I would get. For the entire afternoon, Sandy begged and badgered. Over dinner, I finally relented. "Send me a picture of the lips on your face. My friend wants to see." I thought a clear message was more likely to result in getting what I wanted. When dessert arrived, so did the photograph. It was a close-up of Marti's lips, with a cigarette hanging out.

"A smoker? Yuck. It's just hanging there. Like it's, uh, hmm. That's...that's kind of arty, isn't it? She has nice lips."

Chapter 15

Days were spent walking around Paris and talking about sex. I felt relaxed until I told Sandy, "She makes these circles with her tongue that I swear will make me go blind one day." An elderly woman near us had heard. "You're a disgusting pervert," she said in perfect English. I had forgotten that many people here also spoke English. I was embarrassed until Sandy said, "She teaches blind child victims of war how to speak again with artificial replacement tongues. How is that perverted?" When the woman had no answer to that, Sandy said, "Ah, so you are the pervert here! Let's get away before it rubs off!" She pulled me away. As soon as she turned the corner, she burst out laughing. I was still embarrassed by what I had said in public without realizing.

That night, I sent Marti a message telling her an old woman called me a pervert. She sent a message back. "Is your friend perverting you? I'm sad. Pix please."

"No perversion happening. No pix."

"You perverted me with your panties. I'm going to break into your apartment and steal your undies. Where do you keep your dirty laundry?"

She made me laugh, though I have no doubt she was considering doing just that. "No thievery." Her response was to send me a photo of her butt. She was wearing my underwear. She'd kept the ones I had once shoved in her face, and I found it romantic. I sent back a selfie of my kissing the air and turned in for the night.

On our last morning, Sandy and I were sitting in an outdoor café, La Pâtisserie de la Seine enjoying the sun. I had a Croissant de Brume. The croissant is a delicate pastry with layers of flaky dough enveloping a filling of light vanilla custard infused with hints of rose. Sandy was scrolling through my phone messages with Marti. "Nice butt. She has the same underwear as you, but she needs a smaller size. I still don't see her face, though. Is it because she's ugly?"

"Not ugly," I said absently. Very 'not ugly'. I looked at the custard in the croissant and dipped my finger in, pulling out a good amount of the creamy filling. "Take my picture. Close-up," I said to Sandy as I opened my mouth and stuck my finger in. She took a half dozen. She asked what I was going to write when I sent the photo. I had to think about it. I had time. Our flight didn't leave for another six hours. We wandered a little, checking out dresses and handbags. It took almost an hour, but I finally knew what to say.

"Hot under the sun," I typed, and sent with the custard photo.

"So you have this mystery lover who is so unattractive you don't have any photographs, but who you sext with, and badly I might add, but who you kept secret from me, but who sends you nipple and butt pictures."

"I never said she was unattractive. Where did you get that idea?"

"No photos of her face."

"She's actually quite attractive."

"What's the downside? There has to be a downside."

I really did not want to tell her about Marti's addiction. Sandy knew about Donny and would have something to say about it. "She's a lot more sexually advanced than I am."

"Advanced? That sounds like an upside, not a downside."

"I mean, very advanced. It's a little overwhelming."

"Are you exclusive?"

"No. I don't think she could ever be with just one person. I think she has different lovers for different sexual appetites."

"Ooh, what are you offering?"

"I think I'm as boring as Kevin."

"You have a–"

My phone dinged with Marti's response. She'd wrote, "Wet under the moon." The accompanying photograph was mind-blowing. Marti was standing on her fire escape at night, neon providing the lighting. It was pouring rain. She had a cigarette in her mouth and her eyes were half-closed. She had on only a white tank top, soaked and see-through from the rain. She was bent forward slightly, using both hands to pull down the top to cover her crotch. I could see her breasts clearly: her nipples were hard and her face was orgasmic. I was stunned by the image and my pussy just exploded. I gasped as I felt my panties flood. I'd have been a mess if I had been wearing a dress.

"Oh my God! Billie! She's a goddamn model! She's gorgeous!" Sandy was looking over my shoulder. "She's not a model, she just acts like one sometimes."

"Can I..." Sandy didn't finish her question, but took my phone from my hand. I snatched it back. "I want to see."

"No, it's a rude photo." I wondered who took the photograph.

Sandy pointed to a store display near us. The poster in the window was a naked woman with a cheese wheel held in front of her. "We're in Paris. Nothing is rude." I looked again at the photo, and once again my pussy clenched up. "So, that's your girlfriend?"

"More like, I'm one of her many girlfriends."

"Billie. Billie, Billie, Billie. You have this at home waiting for you, and you're as sexually adventurous as Kevin? No, that won't do. Look. Here's what I need. I need...I need her photo. I need you to be absolutely wild. And I need you to tell me ever-ee-thing-a. In detail. I need this."

Sandy said she wanted to use Marti and me as a fantasy to spice up things for her while Kevin grunted through his routine. She was unabashed in her demands. And quite repetitive. She just kept asking over and over.

I mulled over the request for the entire flight back. Sandy pushed it until I asked that she stop. It was creeping me out. On the last leg of the flight, from Montreal (that's where they speak French) to Toronto, I went as far as telling Marti about Sandy's request. I should have guessed her response. "Fuck yes! Let her jerk off to us! Does she want a close-up of my pussy?" I quickly answered that no close-ups were required.

This was not a role I'd ever played for anyone. While Marti is hot, I am not fantasy fodder. I don't like the idea of someone getting aroused thinking about me. Weird, isn't it? That I don't want people to think I'm sexy? Sandy said she understood and wouldn't ask again. We changed the subject, and for the entire drive from Canada, Sandy chatted about everyday life.

Sandy's children—Evan 12, Sadie 9 and Tally 6—are the loves of her life. She attends parent-teacher meetings, choir performances (though she said Sadie is a terrible singer), and soccer, chess and baseball games. On a weekday, she wakes up at 6 am, spends two hours getting the kids and her husband breakfast and making their lunches, getting their things organized and everyone out the door. Kevin drives the kids to school. She gets to work by 8:45 am, ready to work by 9 am. Half an hour for lunch. Clock out at 5pm, home by 5:45 to start dinner. Kevin would already have picked up the kids and be home, doing homework. On weekends, it was a similar morning routine, but she shuttles the children around to their activities while Kevin works a second job. Once a week, they have perfunctory sex and Sandy pretends to orgasm. Once a month, they visit both sets of grandparents. Rinse and repeat.

I told her about my top twenty placement in the baking competition, the close call I had with Tiffany and the money laundering scheme, and even told her the real reason for the Lavender Bliss cookies. I said I'd met up with Marti at both a hospital and a jail.

"Wait, wait, wait. You have a lover who has this crazy job that gets her beat up and arrested like a spy, but also saves you from a possible federal crime. She adores you so much she sleeps in your doorway and still wants to see you after you kicked her? And she's a smoking hot babe who is great in the sack? I hate you. That's a dream life I want. I'd prefer a hot guy, but hell, I just might take the hot babe."

"I know it sounds pretty exciting, but I left out the boring stuff. Who wants to hear that?"

"You didn't leave it out. You told me all about it already. And besides, I didn't have anything except the boring husband and the boring stuff."

"Kevin isn't that bad."

"Let's compare. I'll message Kevin, you message…what's her name?"

"Marti."

"I'll message Kevin, you message Marti. The message is, 'Almost home. What's up?' And then we'll compare answers."

I agreed, though I warned her that Marti was very likely not to answer. Kevin responded almost immediately: "Yeah! Kids miss you. Pizza tonight?" To my surprise, Marti left a voicemail instead of a message. "I want to wolf down your pussy and fuck you until you faint. I'll be waiting at your place. Don't kick me this time. Bring your friend if you want." She always has to take it one step too far. Sandy laughed it off, but it was embarrassing. By the time we got to my place, and she saw Marti's dark figure smoking in the doorway, a sadness came over her face.

"I wish I had a feral lover waiting in the rain for me." After Marti and I got upstairs, I sent Sandy the photo. Then Marti wolfed me down.

Chapter 16

Sandy went from the phone call once-a-month friend to the phone call every-day friend after our trip. I didn't much care for it. I had other things to do than tell her about my day. But she called me every morning to hear all about my previous day. She was expecting details about my wild sexual escapades, but she got details of what outrageous thing some privileged customer said to my staff, and that the flour delivery was delayed.

But I began to look at my life differently because of those conversations with Sandy. I realized that my life is how I narrate it. It's choosing the stories I tell. Why would I tell her only the boring parts? Why would I deny both her and myself the pleasure of recounting pleasure? And more importantly for me, why shouldn't I be an object of desire? Marti desired me. But why not be desired for my conversation? Desired for telling erotic stories? It was surprisingly fun when I told Sandy about a night with Marti. She was an enthusiastic listener without being creepy. I was relieved and decided I could get used to this. Without Sandy, honestly, this book wouldn't exist.

In an erotic message, I told Marti. "I'm talking about you. I'm telling people you stuck your tongue deep inside my pussy last night. Do you like it?"

"People? Plural? We'll have to start doing more to keep the audience entertained. I want to eat your asshole."

For as audacious as she is, I have thus far refused her access. She kissed my ass once, through my underwear, but I told her to please stay away. She agreed without asking why. She was respectful like that. She said, "Let me know if you change your mind." And I was thinking I might change my mind.

Marti is into almost any kind of sex. Stylistically, she has limits–she once told me she refuses to let both of her hands be bound at once. But I'm talking about reasons for sex. Sad sex, happy sex, pity sex, break-up sex, make-up sex, narcissistic sex, angry sex, charity sex. She's done it all, and she likes it all. Doing anal with her would be curiosity sex. On my part, anyway. While I think her doing it to me would be mind-blowing, I'm just not sure about reciprocating.

When I told Sandy I thought I was too vanilla for Marti, she laughed for a solid two minutes. When she finally caught her breath, she said two things that really hit me: "I think every woman might be too vanilla for her," and "You let her stick her finger in your vagina in a public restaurant, and then turned it into a goddamn cookie! I don't think you're as vanilla as you think."

Chapter 17

Marti and I had our first fight shortly after I returned from Paris. I thought at first that it was minor, a problem that would disappear like cotton candy in the rain. We would have another sip of coffee, a bite of danish, and it would be gone. I was wrong.

It started when she came to the bakery. She ordered her usual and sat at a table, waiting. She liked to sit and watch us work, but that day, she was stoned out of her head. Jean brought her coffee, and as she gently put the cup down, Marti grabbed her hand and kissed it. Jean giggled and smiled and took no offense. Marti smiled back with half-open eyes. Her very sexy look. Jean wanted to take the danish over, but Grace insisted, and snatched the plate from Jean's hand. They had a tense but quiet argument while I was busy serving a customer. I settled it by telling them both to get to work, and I brought Marti the danish and sat down with her.

She smelled like whiskey and smoke. I hated it, but was usually aroused by it. That day, I just hated it. I told her she stank. She bent her head down, sniffed, and shrugged.

I told her she needed to take more pride in how she presented herself. She said there was nothing different today from any other day. Why complain now? I told her this was my place of work, my business, and I did not want her throwing a spanner in the works. She played stupid and asked what a spanner was. I said that wasn't the point. Playing stupid again, she asked what the point was.

She is not a stupid woman, not even when she is wrecked on drugs. Her ingenue act offended me. She had purposely come into my bakery to stir up some shit. I told her that and she said something to me that poured gasoline on the fire: "Calm down."

Calm down? I was calm, but I was angry. And here she is, accusing an angry woman of being hysterical, irrational. She's creating a schism between my very friendly, loyal staff, and she's telling me to calm down. I said, a little loudly, "Don't tell me to calm down!" I told her she was treating me like a hysterical woman, she was embarrassing me and my staff, and it was just plain wrong of her to kiss Jean's hand.

She lit up a cigarette and cocked her head. She said she wasn't disrespectful. She'd kissed the hand of a woman who served her and that unless she had complained, I should mind my own business. I reminded her this is my business, my bakery. My sentences were becoming sharp and loud, while hers were becoming soft and wavy. She was doing it on purpose to highlight her drug use, to make fun of me.

She asked me, "What the fuck is going on here?" I told her if she hadn't been so high, she'd understand perfectly. She kept playing stupid, pretending not to understand. She took a drag of her cigarette, which, of course, infuriated me. "Put that out!" I shouted. When she didn't, I snatched it from her lips and dropped it into her coffee. "No. Smoking."

"What the fuck? You've always let me smoke in here."

"Clearly, if I give you permission once, you just assume it applies forever."

"It isn't once. It's every time. Every single time I come in here, I smoke."

I told her that's not the point. The point was, she just made crazy assumptions about me, that I would always roll over and let her do whatever she wanted, even when she knew it was wrong. She just leaned back in her chair and refused to talk. "You said I could tell you anything, that we should be open and honest with each other. I didn't think you'd act like an asshole when I told you what I really felt."

"I'm not the one who threw a cigarette in my coffee."

"This isn't about cigarettes."

"Is it about raspberry danish? If I eat it, are you going to grab it from me and throw it across the room?" She was treating me like a child, and took a big bite of the danish to make a point. "Take it, I'm done."

No way was she going to dump me like this. "You're done alright! Get out. Now!" I stood up and pointed at the door. She's stood up, pulled her hoodie over her head, and stormed out. She kicked a nearby garbage can as she crossed the street. I was shaking so badly. In less than half an hour, Marti had tried to seduce Jean right in front of me, and caused Grace and Jean to make fools of themselves in front of customers. She came in drunk and stoned and stinking, started smoking right in front of me, talked to me like I was an idiot, and she had the audacity to try to break up with me!

I was furious. Jean and Grace were standing there, staring at me. I told them to bus the damned table and went into the office to find a little peace. It didn't work. I was seeing red. I called and left a message.

"Hey, you know what? Screw you! I can't believe I wasted my time and feelings on a lying, cheating piece of trash like you. You think you can just waltz in and out of my life whenever it suits you, huh? Well, guess what? I'm done with your sorry ass. I saw you with Jean. I know about the drugs and drinking, and I'm not putting up with it anymore. You think you can play me for a fool? You think I'm just gonna sit here and take it? Hell no! You're dead to me now. Don't you dare try to come crawling back, begging for forgiveness, because you won't get it. I deserve better than your lies and your betrayal. So go ahead, keep living your pathetic excuse for a life. But don't you dare think for one second that I'll be waiting for you to come back. I'm done with you. Goodbye, and good riddance!"

I ripped off my apron and headed into the shop. Grace said Marti had left her lighter on the table, and I told her to throw it on my desk. I didn't go home, that was too close and too soon. I went to a bar across the street for a drink and a chance to think. I sat at the bar and ordered a red wine. It seemed like the right choice: nothing too hard, but enough to take my edge off. I chatted to a couple of people at the bar–that's what you do, right? Talk to people to let your anger out? I guess I was a little too intense, because I was soon sitting alone watching the TV. And soon after that, I was not sitting alone but in the company of a very drunk man. I was almost finished with my wine when I got up to use the ladies room. I returned and finished my drink, planning to head home.

I woke up the next morning on the floor of the bakery with a pile of aprons under my head. My head was killing me. How the hell did I get here? Did I stay for another drink–even one was a lot for me–and decide to sleep in the bakery instead of heading upstairs? I was glad the bar was so close. I had zero recollection, and it was a bit disconcerting that I'd left the keys by the door. I must have locked the door and just dropped the keys where I stood.

My back and neck were sore, but I went home and trudge up the stairs to my apartment. It was 4 am. I was going to have to be at work in an hour, so I stepped into the shower. Only while I was washing did I really look at my arms. My wrists and biceps had large bruises on them. The bruise on my right bicep looked like fingers. I managed one more breath before I threw up. I cried and my mind was racing. I couldn't remember anything after going to the ladies room. Nothing until waking up. Was I tied up at the wrists? Held by my arms? Kidnapped? I did a mental check in. I hope you never, ever have to wonder to yourself, "Was I sexually assaulted?"

It took 20 minutes for me to get my shit together enough to get dressed and go downstairs. The bakery has security video. I was stumbling into the shop when my phone rang. Sandy, calling for her morning update. I asked her to come to the bakery, please. Something terrible happened, and I needed her. She was knocking at my door within 15 minutes. She must have sped the entire way and run more than a few red lights.

She held me as I sat trembling, telling her everything. The stupid argument–I knew I had blown it completely out of proportion and made unfair accusations–the voicemail to Marti, the drink, waking up. I showed her my bruises. I threw up in the wastepaper basket. Sandy tied up the bag and threw it in a dumpster out back. By the time she came back, I had cued up the video.

"Are you ready?"

"I don't think I'll ever be ready." I clicked play, then had to fast forward until I saw Marti storm out of the shop and cross the street, then slip down an alley. Later, I walked out. I watched as I walked across the street and walked into the bar. The video showed only the bottom couple of feet of the bar I went to. We watched and waited. We could see feet coming and going. The quality was so poor. I couldn't tell myself from anyone else. Suddenly, a figure appeared from under the camera. A black hoodie under a black leather jacket. The hood was up.

"That's Marti!" I said, jabbing at the screen. "What the hell did she do to me?" I shook as I watched the dark, blurry figure cross the street. We could see only the street, the occasional car, and legs. She approached a couple leaving the bar, talking with them before there's some kind of scuffle. The woman fell to the ground. "No! No!" I shouted, stopping the video playback. I stabbed my finger at the indistinct blob. "That's me. That's my shirt. White with one thick blue stripe." I had been wearing that shirt when I woke up.

"Did she push you down?"

I pressed play. Sandy and I watched as Marti and the man fell to the ground near me, fighting. She got a couple of hits in before he slammed her in the face and she went limp for a split second. There was no sound but the woman—me—I was screaming and reaching out to the pair.

I almost stood up, but fell to my knees. There was a flash of light, and the man, who had been getting the better of Marti, jerked back. He got sloppily to his feet, stumbling, holding his arm, running away.

"Did she just...shoot him?"

I replayed it. "Yes, a little bit." We watched as Marti helped me to my feet, helped me cross the street. Then we disappeared from sight. I burst out in tears, sobbing into Sandy's arms. What kind of monster have I become? She'd saved me from him, shot him, brought me to the bakery and locked me in to keep me safe. She even gave me a makeshift pillow.

I heard from Marti a few days later after leaving a dozen begging voice messages for her. "Stop leaving messages. They're filling up my storage."

I had butterflies the rest of the week. I had so many questions: Why was she at the bakery? Why did she come to the bar? Did she really shoot the man? Why was I left in the bakery? Why can't I remember? Would she forgive me for being so irrationally mad at her?

I was sure she had rescued me from something. I needed to apologize for my cruel words, for my poor treatment of her. After everything I'd done, she still came to my rescue. I owed her.

Chapter 18

I took a taxi to Ravencrook Street. Had to pay ahead, and the driver warned me he'd only stop for five seconds. True to his word, he gave me five seconds to get out before he drove off. I passed by the same drug dealer in the doorway. He gave me a small nod and turned away. I wasn't buying anything. He couldn't care less about me.

I was racked with guilt. I knew why I had behaved badly. She didn't. I knew she behaved nobly toward me, but she rebuffed my messages. I needed to explain myself. I could hear music coming from her apartment, which I thought was strange. I never knew her to listen to music. I knocked. I heard a noise in the apartment, and the door opened.

"Hi." The woman in front of me was not Marti. This woman had brown skin, sepia hair, deep blue lipstick and a white smile. I asked if Marti was around. The woman invited me in. "I'm Faith. That's Eva." Eva was a blonde with very little of her pale white skin showing through her tattoos. She had the largest breasts I have ever seen. She was lying on Marti's bed, masturbating with a vibrator.

I stared.

"Are you going to join us?"

"No. I...No thank you. I'm hoping to talk to Marti." I walked into the middle of a threesome, but was more awed than embarrassed.

"She's on the fire escape."

The drapes were closed, but there was movement, meaning the window was open. Falls City tenements like this have only windowed access to the fire escape, whereas I had a real door. The blonde watched me as I crossed the floor, and I could not take my eyes off her until she started to moan. It was like she was thinking of me as a sexual being. I pulled back the drape. Marti was sitting barefoot in a t-shirt and jeans, smoking. I climbed out the window, but her face soured when she saw me. At first I was pissed. Then I remembered I was the asshole here.

"What the fuck do you want?"

"To apologize, I was a jerk."

"No shit. Get out."

"I want to explain–"

"I don't care what you want. What you want is irrelevant."

"Ten years ago, my brother died of an overdose. Heroin."

"So?"

"Ten years ago last week. The anniversary of his death was the day I yelled at you for being high. I found him dead in his bathroom. Every year, I freak out."

"I'm not him."

"I know. I–"

"And I don't want to be your whipping boy." Whipping boy? How does she even know that phrase? But it was true. I was punishing her for my brother's death, though it has nothing to do with her.

"I saw the video of you rescuing me at the bar." She was silent, waiting, ready to pounce on me again. "Thank you. I treated you like shit and said terrible things, and then you saved me."

"I was looking for my lighter. I thought maybe I'd forgotten it there."

"You did. It's in the office."

"I'll pick it up tomorrow."

The more I tried to explain, to thank, the more irritated she became. I said sorry; she said, who cares? I said thank you for rescuing me; she said she wasn't there for me. I said I care about her; she said she cares about herself too. I couldn't win. She flicked her cigarette off the escape, the bright ember sailing through the night, and went back into the apartment. I stared at the glowing neon signs for a long moment, perplexed and angry, and then crawled through the window.

Eva was still by herself on the bed, watching Faith and Marti, who were standing by the bed, kissing passionately. They'd gone back to having sex. My head spun. My senses were overloading. It smelled like sex, and Eva's moans filled the air. Faith pulled Marti's shirt off and her jeans down and began touching her.

I watched, and I felt jealous and angry and upset and turned on. I didn't move, though my eyes roamed everywhere. Eva's breasts, her vibrator, Faith's fingers, Marti's pussy. I looked into her face. Faith was bringing her to orgasm in front of me. I was left out.

Marti turned and looked at me through hooded eyes, then mouthed, "kiss me." My heart leaped. I kissed her passionately. I licked her lips and sucked her tongue. Her breathing was erratic, her moans erotic. "I'm coming." I was too. Somehow, she was sharing her orgasm with me. A hot flash shot through my pussy. She said something I couldn't quite make out. Her mouth was full of my mouth. She came and came and came as she kissed me. She stumbled back to the bed and sat, still dripping wet. Faith offered me her fingers, and I greedily sucked them.

I came around while this woman's fingers–this stranger's fingers–were still in my mouth. What was I doing? I realized I was having fun.

I left the threesome to their exploits and headed home. I had never felt so scared and so brave in my whole life.

Chapter 19

I bake during the day, sometimes have amazing sex at night, and talk about it in the morning. I was enjoying myself. I knew it couldn't last long. Three weeks after Marti picked up her lighter, she was in a terrible car accident and ended up in the hospital. Again. Lori called to let me know. It was bad enough that she was expected to stay a week.

When I arrived, Lori was hovering like a mosquito. Marti would weakly wave her hand to get Lori to leave, and it never worked. That girl is obsessed.

Marti had picked up a child custody case. The father had snatched two kids and fled to Falls City. Police couldn't locate him, so the mother hired her to find her kids. Marti tracked the dad to a rundown motel. She called police and called the mom. Police arrived and found the kids, but the dad had fled.

"The fucker was sitting in the restaurant across the way and the cops never thought to look," she told me. She'd stuck around until the mom arrived and then she left. As she pulled out of the parking lot, she spotted his "shitty black car." She ran into the restaurant, but he'd seen her and fled. He got into his car, and she went after him. They drove through Falls City and when he slowed down for a red light, she rammed into him. He shot at her, she shot at him, and he drove off. They drove madly through the streets, because "that fucker wasn't getting away," she said.

"I was hauling ass, just fucking zoom zoom between the cars. Went after him onto the highway, ripping along. Then there are two motherfucking trucks side by side, blocking the lanes. He can't get past. I catch up and just bam! He slams on his brakes and I slam into him. I spin into the back of a truck. I spin, catch his car, and we both go off the road."

It was hard for me to imagine driving at a high speed, trying to catch a kidnapper shooting at me and then flying off the road into a ditch and laughing about it. It sounds like a movie. Marti laughed while she was telling me.

"I think it's the painkillers. They're making her loopy," Lori said.

Apparently, Lori didn't know that medical treatment for an addict means different pain meds. No wonder Marti was laughing like a hyena. When another woman came in to see Marti, I stepped out to speak to her doctor, to make sure they'd run a tox screen. They hadn't. He was fuming and immediately ordered the blood test. Her medication changed and I never let on it was me that took away her fun.

I walked back into the room to find her making moves on a nurse. I sat down to watch the show. Watching her hitting on a nurse while lying in a hospital bed with broken bones, black eyes and a catheter was like watching a romance zombie movie. Marti could barely move, and her hands were encased in plastic braces. Tubes everywhere, some delivering life and some draining detritus. She didn't care. It almost didn't matter what the nurse said in response.

"Thanks for all your help. You're an angel. Yes, you are. You work so hard. I'm sorry to add to that burden. Oh yes, I have. That other driver was...wooo. Glad it wasn't that bad. I used to be a homicide detective. I'm used to putting my body on the line for justice. He had kidnapped his children, and didn't like that I found him, so he tried to kill me. Big fail, ha ha! The kids are okay. They're safe with their mom now. Oh c'mon, it's all part of doing the right thing. You know that. Nurses do it too. Maybe not via car crashes, but you put your body on the line every single day. Don't tell me you aren't in pain every day. Do you like chocolate? You do? Perfect. I'm going to buy you some chocolate as a thank you. Oh sure, why not? Unless you'll get in trouble for accepting a gift? I don't want to get you in trouble. Plus, who wants to share? You're the one doing all the hard work. Listen, how about this? A thank you dinner. Oh yes, you do deserve it! Give me your number and we'll get together. Please? Let me treat you as a thank you for all you've done for me, plus you're stuck with me for another week, so I am really going to owe you. Yes? Great. Lori, can you give me my phone, please?"

A master class.

She was in good hands with the doctors, had Lori as her efficient sycophant, and enough money to cover the hospital bill. When yet another woman walked in and gave her a big kiss, I decided the bakery needed me more. I didn't get halfway down the hall before Lori came running after me.

"Marti asked for you to come back."

"Is she okay?"

"Yes. I think she just wants you there."

"She has enough women to keep her company."

"She asked me to bring you back. She hasn't sent me for anyone else."

"You're her secretary, not a labrador retriever. You don't have to do everything she asks you."

"I know that. I'm not an idiot."

Testy.

Back in the room–a private room–Marti told Lori to go home and hit the office the next day. "Make sure Claudia Hampton pays. Get a copy of the police report on the car, contact the insurance company. I need a new car. Not new new, but new to me."

We were left alone. "I'm tired," Marti said.

"You've been through a lot. Go to sleep."

"I don't want you to leave."

"I'll stay."

"Promise?"

"Promise."

"You look amazing."

"Thanks, you don't."

"Fuck me?"

I was slightly offended. She always pushed it. "No."

"My hands are bandaged up. I can't do it myself."

A sad look crossed her face, the same look she had when I gave her my panties. I think she practices it in the mirror.

"Can I please get a sex from you? Just one? One small sex, please."

I burst out laughing. "A sex?"

"A little one. No one will even notice." She was performing another master class. Make a woman feel needed, desired. Make her laugh, present yourself in need of her help, make the help seem easy to do. She asked for a kiss, and I gave her one. She asked if I could stand closer to her, so she could "pretend I'm in a field of lavender." I did her one better. I slipped my hand into my pants, pushing aside the cotton panties, and dipped one finger inside. I offered my finger to her. She closed her eyes, opened her mouth, and slightly extended her tongue, like she was taking holy communion. I gently put my finger in her mouth and she suckled until I withdrew it.

"Love you."

My heart hammered in me. She said she loved me. Does she really? Is it the medication? Is that what she said to me the night of the three-plus-one kiss? Do I love her?

"I love you too. Go to sleep. I'll be here when you wake up."

It was a nice room with a private bathroom and shower. Twelfth floor. The chairs were very comfortable, and I suspected, easy to sleep in. When the nurse came in–different from the other one–I asked where I could get coffee and a bite to eat. She said I'd find a room service menu in the pocket in the back of the chair. I should press 9 on the room phone, and she recommended the Valencian paella with chicken, avoid anything with seafood. And don't give any to the patient. I ordered a black coffee and a chicken salad sandwich. It had walnuts.

The view was stunning. I could see across Woodman River and the fast-flowing waters that feed all three falls. Tourists ride glammed-up tug boats in the roiling waters at the base of the falls. Everyone is hoping to spot a floater in the water and post the video to social media before the body is retrieved. Further down, you can take a coal mining car down a steep incline to see the raging water up close. Even the river is violent in Falls City.

Chapter 20

We went for dinner a month after she got out of the hospital. Her right ankle still had a metal brace, so she took a taxi to my place. I got in, and we headed to the restaurant. She was almost in the middle of the back seat and there was barely room for me. "Hey." That was all she said. I asked, "Everything okay?" She nodded and stared straight ahead. I had no idea what was going on, so I just sat and stared at her. She turned, winked, and turned back. She stretched out her hand and tapped her fingers on my knees. I looked at her hand, then at her face. She was still looking ahead, but the corner of her mouth curled up in a grin. She pulled my knee toward her a little and ran her hand along the inside of my thigh. A thrill shot through my body. I quickly looked at the driver. He was too busy driving through the stormy night traffic to pay attention to the two passengers sitting unmoving in his back seat. I checked for a security camera and saw none.

Straining upon the start, the game's afoot.

I looked straight ahead with a straight face and parted my legs for her. She found her way up, pushing my dress. I had to subtly raise my hips so she could push it higher, reach higher. Her fingers brushed my panties and began to stroke me through the cloth. My pussy clenched as if it was trying to grab her fingers as she rubbed. I cleared my throat to hide a gasp as she pinched my clit. She pressed a finger into me; the cloth soaking up my wetness as she wiggled her finger. She withdrew her hand, leaving my panties bunched inside me. I discreetly pulled them out as she licked her fingers. I was both happy and disappointed to get to the restaurant.

"How have you been?" We were standing outside the restaurant, huddled under an awning, waiting to get in. We had reservations, but the group in front of us did not and they were arguing with the host. Marti lit a cigarette and blew smoke toward them in a favorite passive-aggressive move of hers. I told her I'd been alright, working the bakery as usual. Sandy's birthday had just passed.

"Is she the one who wanted the photo?"

"Yes."

"Does she want more?"

"She'd probably be happy to get some, but I'm not in-terested in sharing." I squeezed Marti's arm. "I share you enough."

"Never enough. Hey! We have reservations! Can we just cut through this bullshit?" We could just cut through the bullshit. Marti flicked her cigarette on the ground near one man's feet while I just smiled politely at all the angry glares. It made me feel good to walk past them.

We stepped through and I was dazzled by the lights and sounds. The restaurant was buzzing. Gleaming white tablecloths, gleaming white wait staff uniforms, gleaming white walls with no artwork. I did not like the place. Too sterile for eating. Marti led me to a small area where I could check my coat. "Why didn't you even wear a coat?" I asked. "I have my leather jacket. I didn't want to wear it here. Seems a little too street for this place." She was right. "Don't you have other jackets? Like a raincoat?" She scrunched up her face and shook her head. "Well, every good private detective needs a trench coat. I'm going to buy one for you. We don't want you getting wet all the time." She leaned over and whispered, "Yes, yes, we do."

We sat at a table in the middle of the floor. There would be no touching in this restaurant. Not at the table, anyway. We ordered our drinks quickly. I opted for a glass of white wine, and Marti asked for a double whiskey with a beer back. "Yes, I'm still drinking," she said. I saw no reason for her to announce it. She ordered three drinks at once. It was clear she was still drinking. "But I've been off Shadow for two weeks," she added brightly.

"That's quite a while. How have you been?"

"Alive." Marti started taking about a case she'd just finished. She had been hired by a concerned father whose daughter was going to marry a man he didn't like. He paid Marti $50,000 to find out where the man went when his phone chirped. The special notifications came in at all hours, and the man would drop whatever he was doing and leave. He refused to say where he was going or what was going on. The father assumed it was drugs or an affair. She sat in her car for two days, following the target from his house to his work to his house again. Then he sneaked out at 4 am. She talked about how she struggled to stay sober while doing the boring stuff. "I was told he left the house every day at 6am, though he works nine to five at his future father-in-law's company. You can never rely completely on the information you get, so I camped out and watched him 24/7. It was boring as shit for hours before he left."

She said while waiting she saw a kid sneak out of the window of another house. But since that was not what she was there for, "and I have no idea if they live there or are trying to get out without being noticed, or away from a terrible home life," she did nothing. She noted the address and took photos, just in case the midnight run went sideways. I was touched by her concern for a kid she didn't know.

"At 4 am, this guy literally tiptoes down the front steps. I slide down below the level of the dash. My camera is up and click, click, click. A car comes creeping down the street, lights off, and picks him up. I start the car, lights off, and follow at a distance." She lit a cigarette and polished off her drinks, then signaled for another round.

"Not for me. I've barely started. I'd love to order food, though." When the wait staff arrived, I ordered the dinner salad, while she ordered a club. She had a big drink from her whiskey. She said she followed the car thirty miles to a small park in the middle of nowhere.

"I pulled over and turned off my lights. Watched them park and get out and just...stand there. I've got my camera, taking photos, when knockknockknock. Someone is knocking on my window. Scared the shit out of me. I'm trying to figure out how the fuck I'm going to explain myself. This middle-aged woman is there standing smiling and says 'Hello and welcome, fledgling!'"

"Fledgling?"

"It turns out they're bird watchers. Including my target. It's totally normal for me to have parked down the road, turned off my lights, and taken photos, if I was also bird watching. So Mary and I–that's her name–walk quietly into the park. There's a half-dozen people standing still, looking at the tall grass. Cameras and binoculars up, everyone is whispering about the fucking bird that is in the grass. Some rare something something. A Henslow's Sparrow. A fucking bird."

The target was a birder who would sneak out to meet up with the group to spot rare birds. Secrecy was required to keep the locations unknown by others. She talked a little to every member, making sure her target was, indeed, a longtime birdwatcher. She looked at people's apps and journals which people created and used to one-up each other. This included dates and times for her target. He had 312 birds listed. Marti laughed as she told the story. "This guy paid me 50 crisp to find out his daughter is engaged to a nerd."

I had finished my salad and half a glass of wine. Marti had two more double shots of whiskey with beer chasers, and the toast and bacon from her club. "Not hungry?" Marti pushed her plate away. "Not really. But I like toast."

She doesn't eat properly and probably hasn't for years. She forgets to bathe, she forgets to wash her clothes, she forgets to sleep. She needs someone to drag her into normalcy every once in a while, a way to reset. Don never had that. My family couldn't handle his violent outbursts and his thieving, so we couldn't provide him with much support. Not everyone wants support. I don't know if Marti wants support. She probably doesn't know either.

"If you're making $50,000 for a simple case like that, why do you live in a dump?" I wasn't happy that she laughed at my question. "High medical bills and drugs are expensive. When I'm using, I mean."

"How much for the car crash hospital bill?"

"Not sure. Lori's handling all that shit. I think around $5 million. She'll negotiate it down. Probably to $1 million."

"She's negotiating your medical expenses?"

"Oh hell yes. Question every single line item on the bill. This boot," she said, shaking her foot, "was $15,000 plus $1,000 for a fitting. She asked them to give her the report on the fitting and there wasn't one. They just charge shit and hope you don't look. There was a $200 charge for some fucking sandwich I never had." Holy crap! That was not a $200 sandwich, it was a $2 sandwich. With walnuts. I didn't tell her I ate it. The hospital can track me down if they really want their money.

"You really trust your secretary, hmm?"

"Yeah. She's got a Master's degree or something. She takes directions well. Figures stuff out. Smart kid."

"You know, she's hot for you."

"Who isn't, Baby?"

"I'm serious. You should have seen her at the hospital."

"I've learned my lesson. No fucking the secretary. That cost me a ton of money. And kind of ruined Susan."

"How do you know Lori won't steal from you?"

"I don't."

Chapter 21

I settled the bill after a faux argument with Marti about who should pay, and we got my coat. "I'm going to get you a nice trench coat to keep you dry. I didn't know how you've managed so far without one." Marti scoffed and shook her head. "I like my leather jacket. It's waterproof, you know." No amount of reason could move her toward a long coat, hat, or umbrella. "I'll just leave it somewhere."

As we got into a taxi, she said she'd keep her hands to herself. When I asked why, she said she knows the other driver and trusts him not to look. She knows a half dozen drivers who work in her neighborhood. "Once you find a good driver, you keep them. They can get you out of some crazy situations and they don't ask questions." I didn't want to know what those situations were.

"Hey, this is a date, right?"

"Yes, I think so. Why?"

She tapped away at her phone for a moment, then nodded. "Driver, head to the top of Chats Falls." The driver did what Marti asked. She said it was a hotel with a romantic view. I doubted she knew what the average woman thought was romantic. I pictured a terrible view and cheap motel that sold sex toys from a vending machine and had a lube dispenser by the bed. A place where you have to pay extra to have them turn off the cameras in your room. She laughed when I told her. I think the driver did too.

We arrived. There was a stunning boutique hotel, The Flagstone, was adorned with weathered stone walls and expansive windows, overlooking the natural surroundings. It was like we weren't in Falls City anymore. A winding stone pathway lead us through a lush garden to the grand entrance, where a wooden porte-cochère welcomed us. I picked up a little French while in Paris, I guess.

Stepping into the understated elegance of the lobby, I was in awe. The interior boasts high vaulted ceilings adorned with intricate wooden beams, while soft ambient lighting casts a warm glow over plush furnishings and rich tapestries. A crackling fireplace beckons guests to linger, its flickering flames casting dancing shadows across the polished hardwood floors.

The reception desk, crafted from dark mahogany wood, stands as a centerpiece of the space, manned by attentive staff ready to cater to every whim. Artisanal décor accents the walls, showcasing local artwork and handcrafted pottery, while floor-to-ceiling windows offer breathtaking views of the cascading waterfall outside.

Marti spoke with the concierge, showed her phone, and got a passkey. "Best view," she said. We lingered for a few moments before the concierge said the room was ready.

Ascending the staircase to the top floor–there were only two–we were greeted by the hotel's pièce de résistance: the premier suite. It is the only suite on the floor. Inside was pure luxury, carefully appointed and meticulously designed. A king-sized canopy bed takes center stage, adorned with plush linens and oversized pillows for the ultimate in comfort. There were red rose petals on the bed and an ice bucket holding a bottle of champagne at the foot.

Floor-to-ceiling windows frame panoramic vistas of Chata Falls. The glass is one way. A private balcony with a hot tub offers the perfect spot to unwind and soak in the sights and sounds of the cascading waters below. "Soundproof, too," Marti said, taking my coat and hanging it in the closet. It would seem she did, in fact, know about romance. I was nervous: I'd not seen this side of her, and wondered, "Why now?"

"You're blushing," she said as she brushed my hair back. "What are you thinking that's got you blushing?"

"What you're going to do with me?"

"Mmm. What am I going to do with you?" she asked as she wrapped her arms around my waist. She kissed me, and I savored her probing tongue. She tasted smokey, like whiskey. "You're going to make me scream and shake." As she kissed me, I felt her hand move as she unzipped her pants.

"Kneel in that chair, grab the back," she ordered. She came up behind me and pushed my dress up and my head down. She pulled my panties off and tossed them on the desk, then lowered herself to my pussy. She licked me with long, hard strokes, ending just short of my butt. She is respectful of my boundaries. Her tongue was magical. I started to moan and shiver. "Up you get," she suddenly said, breaking the spell.

She sat on the chair and motioned for me to lie on the floor in front of her. "Closer, legs up here." I laid on the floor, my shoulders on the warm carpet, my torso against her legs, my legs in the air. She grabbed both ankles and spread me apart, then supported my thighs with her hands. Open to her insatiable mouth, I quivered as she bent over and indulged. She sucked and slurped, then suddenly tossed my legs to the side.

"Eat me," she demanded, shifting forward on the chair. I scrambled to my knees, put my head between her thighs, and took her lips into my mouth. She was slick. I wanted to bring her to orgasm in a way she would squirt on my face. I sucked her labia into my mouth. First one side, then the other, using my lips to protect her clit as I bit. She moaned and pulled my head closer. I sucked her clit, pulling it into my mouth and releasing it, over and over, my lips over my teeth. She was delicious, and saliva dripped out of my mouth and between her legs. I got eager and accidentally pulled my lips back, brushing my teeth against her clit. She gasped and jerked. I did it again, and again she gasped and jerked.

"Take your dress off," she said, pushing my head away. I unzipped and let it drop to the floor. When I turned around and bent down to pick it up, she was on me. She put her hands on my shoulders and her hips against my butt. I felt her coarse pubic hair on my ass as she slipped one hand down and fingered me from the front. I screamed louder than I expected, and her expert technique brought orgasm after orgasm. I felt light-headed both from pleasure and from having my head down for so long.

Finally, she moved us over to the bed. The rose petals stuck to our sweaty bodies, and I laughed as I plucked one from her thigh. She kneeled over me and lowered her wet pussy onto my face. She worked her clit while I worked her slit, and she came on my face, gasping and bucking.

She fucked me with her fingers. After I came, while still breathing heavily, she bent down and kissed me tenderly, just once, between my legs. She got up, pulled the duvet over me, and slipped in beside me. She lit a cigarette, her first since we got here. Just as I had asked, she made me scream and shake. I lay curled up with my back to her, but using her arm as a pillow, and watched Chata Falls. The view was stunning.

At one point in the night, I got up to pee. I saw Marti in the hot tub. She drank from the champagne bottle and took a hit of Shadow. I used the bathroom, then went back to bed. I turned away from her and fell back to sleep.

Chapter 22

It was no surprise I woke up before her. I showered and ordered breakfast: eggs, toast, fresh strawberries, and whipped cream. The toast was for Marti. I was almost finished with the eggs when she woke up. She stood naked in front of the window, looking at the Falls, smoking. She said she'd eat later. I selected a strawberry, scooped some whipped cream onto it, and went to her. I opened my robe and pressed myself against her back, slipping one hand onto her belly as I brought the strawberry to her lips. "Lick the cream before you bite," I told her. She wrapped her lips around the strawberry and sucked off the whipped cream before taking the berry into her mouth. She smacked her lips as she ate. I fed her a half dozen strawberries this way and felt good to get vaguely healthy food into her. I tucked my face into her back to hide my tears.

"You okay?" she asked. I distracted her by massaging her clit. I stroked her, feeling her get warmer and swollen. She was soaking. I was getting there. I watched her face in the glass. Her eyes were closed, her lips parted. I stuck my fingers inside her, then held them to her lips for her to suck. She put her cigarette out and splayed herself on the bed. I climbed on top of her, my hand teasing her while I kissed her passionately. She started moaning as I sped up my hand, flicking and squeezing her into a frenzy. She gushed as she orgasmed over and over, leaving a huge wet spot on the duvet. I suggested she move, but she was happy to just lie in it.

We still had the room for under an hour. I fed her toast in bed, deciding the crumbs would be the least of the cleaner's concerns. I ran my fingers from scar to scar, tracing her paths of pain. The rough circle from a gunshot, the almost completely faded thin white line of a knife wound, a jagged scar on her knee from a fall. The car crash scars were healing nicely. Her hands were rough, her thighs were smooth. She has a slim line of downy soft, almost invisible hair from her navel to her thick, curly pubic hair. It was delightfully simple, soft, natural. She has an air of confident sexuality. If I had that line of hair, I'd have shaved it off. On her, it was just part of her unruliness.

I had a strange moment of lightheadedness. It was hard to believe I had this smutty, mouthwatering woman at my fingertips. I was a dumpy kid. I am a dumpy woman. I'm alright with that. More than alright with it thanks to this beast lusting after me. I asked if my looks were a problem, and did she want me to lose some weight? "Do you re-member when we first met? Way back, when I arrested that guy and trashed your store? And I bit into that danish? The look on your face..."

"I was scared you'd really hurt yourself."

"No, you weren't scared. You were upset. You were concerned I'd hurt myself. Distressed. About me. Nobody gave a fuck if I was hurt. Except you. That look. And then when I said I was joking, you looked relieved. Like you cared. I know it took a while to come back–"

"Four years."

"Yeah, well, bad shit happened. And when I came back four years later, your face was just as beautiful. Bright and happy and you remembered me."

"You are memorable."

"And every time you look at me, I see that you care. Of course your looks matter, that look matters, the look of caring. I see that in your face. I mean, except when you kick me." She is never going to let me live that down. That's okay. She sees me. We had just minutes to vacate the room, and I roused her out of bed. She'd snatched my panties before I had a chance to put them on, and I was perversely pleased. We headed to the lobby to check out, and I summoned a taxi while she paid the bill. Looking around, I knew I would never have been able to afford it.

As we waited, she asked if the evening had been romantic enough for me. It sure had. "I can't promise to do that often. You know I'm unreliable and fucked up. But maybe we can come back another time?" she asked. We never did.

A couple of weeks later, Marti messaged me, asking if I would meet her at the Frostbite Lounge. I had to look it up. It was a sketchy queer bar in a sketchy part of town. When I protested, she promised it was an oasis in the city, and had never had any serious crime. I relented and took a taxi. It was a dump. The music was so loud it made my head throb.

I walked in and it was poorly lit and stank of booze and cigarettes. Exactly the kind of place Marti would like. I looked around for her, and finally spotted her at the bar. A blonde was whispering, or maybe shouting, in her ear. I walked up beside her and waited for the blonde to be finished. When it seemed to take more than a minute, I poked her in the side. She turned and smiled lazily. She was high, drunk, and barely coherent. The blonde was not happy she'd lost Marti's attention and tapped her shoulder. Marti shrugged her off and instead lit a cigarette. "Gimme sec," she said as she downed half her whiskey.

The blonde squeezed herself into the space between me and Marti to continue her seduction. Marti was perturbed. "Hey, hey. I'm with her," she mumbled, pointing at me. The blonde gave a dismissive look down her nose. "No way you are. I'm much prettier," she said to Marti.

"You're confusing 'pretty' with 'pathetically desperate for attention.'" Her comment made me snicker, and it almost made the blonde give up. She put both arms around Marti's neck and tried to kiss her. Marti pushed her away and pulled her gun. "Fuck off," she growled. The blonde screamed and fled, and the gun was quickly holstered. I was stunned. She swayed a little, blinked, and her face lit up like I'd just arrived. "Let's go." She stumbled toward the door, where the blonde was talking to the bouncer and crying.

The bouncer put out her hand to stop Marti, but she just walked right past and out the door. That was the end of it. With her outside the club, the bouncer didn't care.

But I cared, and that wasn't the end of it for me. I wasn't sure what I should do, since grabbing her could get me shot. I followed her as she lurched down an alley, careening off walls and dumpsters before stopping in a doorway. She slowly slid to the ground, eyes closed, and passed out. It started to rain, and I stared at her for a few minutes. I was angry at the junkie who threatened someone with a gun. I was scared for the woman blacked out in an alley. I had nothing for her but emotion, and right now, emotions were useless. I turned and walked away.

I got a call from her secretary the next morning, asking me if I was okay. Marti recalled leaving me at a bar. I asked why Marti wasn't the one calling, and Lori explained Marti had fallen asleep on the couch after asking her to call me. I wondered if she was being a coward, but decided she was just being an addict. I said I was fine.

I told everyone who asked not about the hotel, not about the good stuff, but about the bar, only the bad stuff. Sandy was aghast, Grace and Jean perplexed. No sugar coating it. Sandy took it hard. Clearly she'd built some fantasy in her head, and this was ripping it apart. I'd warned her. I think. Grace was sad. Jean was confused. How do you love someone who is uncontrollable, disappoints you, and seems to care more about their drugs than you? What do you do when they seem proud of their addictions? Despite the hurt I knew was coming–my brother died of a drug overdose after all–I haven't given up on her. I'm still looking for a way through.

Marti happily admits her sex addiction. She is unashamed of her drug and alcohol addictions. She probably isn't even aware of her adrenaline addiction and her addiction to risk. I'm not sure I've seen the complete picture of her damage. I doubt I've seen the complete picture of her attempts to heal herself.

I live with the uncertainty. She may call, or not. She may make a date, or not. She may be dead in a dirty back alley, or not. I can't control her. Hell, I can barely control myself sometimes. I've never been one of those "be mindful and meditate" people, and I'm not alone in that. I just say "fuck it" and let it go. We all die. Life is uncertain. Death is not. I read once that when you stop being afraid of death and loss, only then can you fully live and fully love. I hope so, but I'm still scared. I won't be able to do this forever, but maybe I can do it for long enough.

Chapter 23

The drug trade in Falls City is going strong, and every corner of the city is touched in one way or another. I think Falls City was built on heroin, coke, Wunk, MethLumina and Shadow. So I shouldn't have been surprised when I received a call from Marcus Thornfield for catering. What did surprise me is that it was for a funeral.

I couldn't believe my ears when I heard Marcus's name. His reputation as a ruthless crime boss involved in the city's seedy drug underbelly was well known. He ran one of the top three crime syndicates in Falls City, or so says the newspapers on an almost daily basis. My heart raced as I listened to his request.

"Ms. River, I need your services for the wake for Harvey Finestone. I know he loved your bakery," he said, his voice low and gruff. Harvey was an older man who came into the bakery three times a week. He would have a pumpkin spice tea and a Lavender Bliss cookie. If no table was available, we would pull a table and chair from the back and set it up for him. He'd been a regular since before I started working there. He was pleasant, and I thought he was a retired accountant. When Marcus called, it put Harvey in a whole new light.

"Harvey's funeral? Of course, Mr. Thornfield. What do you have in mind?" I hadn't heard how Harvey died. Anything was possible. But I knew better than to ask questions, especially from Marcus Thornfield.

He proceeded to give me the details: 200 expected guests with another caterer providing small sandwiches. There would be alcohol. "Don't run out of food. Don't make me look cheap." He settled on 600 Lavender Bliss cookies and 30 two-layer chocolate cakes. We started organizing right away. Grace would help me, and Jean would handle the store. I was grateful I own a double rack oven.

We threw ourselves into the work, making the cookies first. The sweet scent of sugar and the sharp tang of bergamot filled the air, mingling with the underlying tension that hung over us like a cloud. Marti left me a dirty message, which I picked up during a bathroom break. "I want to lick your cream before I bite your berry." My pussy desired her, but I had no time. I didn't call back. The cookies were done quickly enough. It was the cakes that would take all the time. And the longer the ovens were in use for the cakes, the less time for baking the standard store offerings.

As we worked, the rain began to pelt against the windows of the bakery, a steady drumbeat that seemed to match the rhythm of our hands. The storm clouds had rolled in quickly, casting an eerie darkness over the city. I sent the girls home and kept working through the night. I set alarms for myself to make sure I wouldn't fall asleep. Even a five-minute nap could result in an over-baked cake. No way did I want to risk that. We managed to get everything made, tasted, iced, and packaged in time. Each one was a work of art, a final tribute to Harvey.

After placing the last cookie carefully into the box, we loaded everything into the van. Jean climbed into the back, wedging herself around the cakes to keep them steady. Grace slid into the passenger seat, and we headed off.

I followed the NAV directions, having never been to this convention center. The windshield wipers struggled to keep up with the downpour. The world beyond the glass was a blur of gray.

We arrived 2 hours before the wake. A van for Benny's Baguettes was parked near the rear door. That must have been where Harvey spent the other portion of his time. There was a man in a suit standing at the loading dock doors. He looked like a Secret Service Agent. He never spoke, but nodded and opened the doors for us. We parked and quickly unloaded the cakes and cookies.

It took us an hour to set everything up. I was grateful to see the venue staff were well organized and had servers on hand who would cut and serve the cakes. The cookies were set up so anyone could take them. The light scent of sugar clung to my fingers like an erotic reminder of their inspiration.

I was putting the finishing touches on the cakes, fixing little mishaps in the icing, when I felt someone reach past me to the cookies. Rude! I gave them a sharp jab in the ribs with my elbow and they grunted. I recognized the grunt.

"What was that for?" Marti asked, rubbing her side. She had a cookie in her hand and a pout on her lips.

"What are you doing here?"

"I knew Harvey, the dead guy."

"I know who he is. He was a regular at the bakery."

"Harvey? I'd never have imagined."

"How did you know him?"

"One of my dealers," she whispered as she took a bite of cookie. "Mmm. Delicious. You know what this reminds me of?"

"I have to work. Go away."

"Not without an apology."

"For what?"

"You jabbed me in the ribs. You're always hurting me."

Not as much as you're hurting me, I thought. "Sorry. I have just a few minutes to finish up."

"Cool, see you," she said as she pinched my butt and walked away. She didn't return. Jean, Grace and I finished up. More people were arriving. The women were dressed to the nines, and men were wearing suits and ties. Others were in more casual clothes–sweaters and khakis, business casual. I briefly wondered if everyone except us was involved in drugs somehow. We headed out and spent the drive back to the bakery gossiping about who we had seen.

I was exhausted. I had a bubble bath and slept late the next day.

Chapter 24

When I heard the message from Marti, I sighed. "I want to fuck you under bright lights so I can see every glistening drop of you." She knew what would turn me on. I sat for a moment, imagining her animal eyes watching every movement, every twitch of my body. I called and left a message. "I want to dominate you and make you beg to eat me." I was shocked I'd said that, but it was true. I had learned a lot from her about being confident enough to fantasize. I wondered if she had learned anything from me. Maybe how to eat strawberries.

"I am begging you. Make me eat your ass." Whoo! I could hear her hunger in that message. I felt a surge of desire, a surge of power. Maybe I already dominated her. That thought made me laugh for a solid five minutes. But the more I thought of it–and I did spend an inordinate amount of time daydreaming about controlling her–the more I wondered if I might be able to do it. She makes me understand why people think lions and tigers would make great pets, and why that's never really a good idea. But if I was to try, how would I do it? She has a compelling energy about her which I did not. When she said "lick this, suck that," I did what I was told. When I said the same thing in my head, it sounded weak and timid. A question, not a demand. Still, the thought of controlling her, even for an hour, was exhilarating. My phone dinged. Another voice message.

"I've been lying on my bed, thinking of you. Imagining you over me, your pussy just out of reach until you tell me to move. To lick and suck and fuck. Waiting for you to let me move." My hand was trembling when I hung up. She was so good at manipulation, she could insist that I dominate her, and I felt like I had to. I wanted to. I needed to.

I left a message for her. "I'll be there in an hour. Don't move until I get there."

I told the girls I was calling it an early day at the bakery, grabbed a danish, and I went home. My head was spinning and my legs were weak. I stood in front of my closet. What do you wear to a domination? I didn't have the wardrobe for anything stereotypical. No black leather, no high heels, no kinky masks. I started with my panties and built my outfit from there. I selected a thin silver thong I rarely wore. They were so slim, my pussy hung out on either side. The V at the back was just a little bigger. Next, I chose a matching silver bra — I'm grateful that lingerie is often sold as a set.

I chose a light purple velvet dress. The back plunged deeply, and the side slit came up to my mid-thigh. I stepped into it and wiggled it up my body. My black kitten heels went perfectly with the ensemble. It took me 15 more minutes to decide on my bland beige trench coat. It would cover me when out in public, no problem, and it offered an exciting reveal. I messaged her: "I'll be there in 20 minutes. Wear jeans, boots, white tank top, black leather jacket." She looked good in that outfit.

I took a taxi, repeating over and over to myself, "Do what I say." By the time I arrived, I'd found just the right tone. I didn't care if the driver heard me mumbling to myself.

I dashed quickly out of the rain and into the building. There was no damned way I was going to let the rain ruin my hair and makeup. That guy was nowhere to be seen. I trembled a little as I walked up the stairs. Do I knock? Pound on the door? Call out? I'm sure her neighbors must be used to the sounds coming from her place.

I stood in front of the door, steeled myself, and tested the handle. Open. I walked in. Marti was slouched in a chair, smoking, a carnivore resting before the hunt. "Shut the door." She raised a quick eyebrow and got up to lock the door. I raised my arms out. "Take my coat." She smiled and undid the belt on the trench coat, undid the buttons, and opened it. "You're beautiful." She took the coat and slung it over the chair.

As her eyes roamed, her nipples got hard. So did mine. I sat and stretched out a leg, wiggling my foot. "Take my shoes off." She kneeled in front of me, head bowed, as she undid the straps and took my shoes off. I crossed one leg over the other and pushed my bare foot toward her. "Use your mouth." She took my foot in both hands and raised it to her lips. She kissed and licked each foot, running her tongue between my toes and caressing my ankles. I pulled my foot back and put it on her chest. I pushed, and she sat back on her haunches. "Pull up a chair, sit down." She did. She was so damned attractive with that half grin on her face. I was grateful I had a high slit in the dress, as it enabled me to straddle her lap. I kissed her, running my hands through her hair, down her breasts, down her stomach. "Tickle my pussy," I told her. As we kissed, she slipped her hand along my thigh and between my legs. I felt her thighs move under me as she rubbed me.

I stood up. "Give me your jacket. I want to wear it." Marti loved that jacket. It was like a second skin. I'd never tried it on before. Marti paused and frowned a little. "Do what I say." It sounded powerful, just as I had practiced. She stood up and put the jacket on me. It was heavy, enveloping. It smelled of sex and sweat and desire. I pulled her tank top up and feasted on her breasts. I pulled open the button on the top of her jeans, then pulled the zipper down. I could see a small bit of white cotton: her under-wear. She swallowed hard and her breath got a little heavier. I was getting wet and wondered if she was too. I shoved my hand down her jeans and stroked her underwear along the crotch. I pushed the tip of my finger into her, also pushing in her underwear, as she had once done to me.

"Take your jeans off. I want to see if you're wet." Once her boots and jeans were off, she stood in a pair of white cotton underwear. She spread her legs so I could see they were damp and slightly see-through. She drew a sharp breath and said, "Please fuck me."

"Oh, I will. Sit on the edge of the bed," I said as I turned my back on her. "Lift up my dress. Tell me what you see. Get nice and close." I was excited and wondered if I'd soaked through my thong. She lifted the back of my dress as I bent over.

She moaned a little. "I see your beautiful ass and a silver thong. It goes right up the crack." I felt her shift, and I spread my legs so she could get closer. I heard her swallow as she looked. "I see your pussy lips. They're wet and swollen. The thong is soaked." She took a deep breath. "You smell so good." I could feel her hot breath near my pussy. Then she ran her face up along the crack of my ass, almost touching, but not quite. "Take my panties off." I could feel her hands shake as she pulled them off.

"Do you like them?"

"Yes."

"Do you want to kiss them?"

"Yes, please." When she said "please", my pussy clenched. I told her to kiss and suck the crotch. I watched as she passionately kissed my panties, and she watched as I shrugged off the jacket and pulled the dress from my shoulders. It fell to the floor. I was feeling bold. I told her to stop, and to choose her favorite toy from her sex toy box. I stroked my breasts and pinched my nipples. "Take that off, put those on." She took off her underwear and put her boots back on.

Grabbing a pillow from the bed and throwing it on the floor, I laid down. "Stand over me." She paused for a moment. "Do what I say." Her boots stomped next to my head, one of the laces flicking against my cheek. It sent a shock through my body. I wasn't sure where this was coming from: I had no special love for her boots.

Standing over me, I watched as she poured lube on the toy—a rabbit vibrator. She dropped a remote control onto my chest. She rubbed the vibrator on herself as foreplay before slipping it in. I clicked the remote, and it turned on, clicked it again, and the pattern of the vibrator changed. She moaned as she pressed it against her G-Spot and the silicone ears around her clit. By the fourth click of the remote, I had found her preferred setting. She came as I watched from below, and it was beautiful and arousing.

We moved to the bed where she worked my pussy with her mouth. She sucked and licked. My body pulsated, and I shivered as I came. I demanded she kiss me, and she brought her wet lips to my mouth, pushing her tongue in deeply. I tasted my pleasure. "Up here. Touch yourself. Come on my face," I said.

Obediently, she scrambled up and rubbed her clit. I grabbed her ass to move her into a more favorable position and took the opportunity to touch her asshole. It was the first time I had ever done that, and she moaned and moved back, moving against my finger.

"Back into position!" I stroked her hole, and she moved forward. With the extra stimulation, when she came, she squirted onto my face. I drank in the rain from heaven. I pulled her down onto my face to lap up the last few drops.

We went all night long. Fucking her, fucking me, fucking each other. We opted to shower together, and she ate me with water streaming down her face. We returned to bed and only then did I remember the raspberry danish I'd brought for her. She fetched it from the pocket of my coat. It was stuck to the paper bag, but Marti simply ripped the bag open and licked it to get to the filling. She was beside me in bed, smacking her lips and feeding me the occasional morsel. I fell asleep listening to her lick her fingers clean.

It was a blast trying to dominate Marti. I say 'try' because it's like trying to dominate a hurricane. With Marti, every once in a while, she would give me a bemused look. An expert putting up with a novice. It is exhausting thinking up all the things to do. I surprised myself with my own suggestions and arousals. I felt safe with her, open to my own desires.

Chapter 25

In the early morning, I looked at Marti as she slept. She had the body of a junkie who hadn't gone too far down. Little fat is left on her frame, and her body hasn't fed on the muscle yet. Yet. My Donny had gone too far. He was skeletal. I always wondered: if he had a healthier body, could he have survived the overdose? When he died, he left me with that question. My mycelium made me feel like I was doing something to help the future Dons who might survive with a little more health.

Marti's breathing was deep and steady as she slept. I noticed a Shadow inhaler on the table that hadn't been there the night before. I got dressed and retrieved my coat. I gave her a kiss before I left, light and tender. She stirred, but stayed asleep. I got home, showered and changed, and headed to the shop. I didn't have time to chat with Sandy, so I ignored her call and sent a "Sorry! So busy!" message. Grace had done the morning bake and Jean had opened. I was grateful for those two.

In the basement of the bakery, I turned on the mushroom light. Setting up the environment had been no small feat. I converted a corner of the bakery into a mushroom cultivation chamber, complete with temperature and humidity controls. It hadn't taken long to find the perfect settings: knowledge about the effects of temperature and humidity is key as a baker, especially in the ever-damp atmosphere of Falls City.

The mycelia spread and colonized the substrate well, and some of the mushrooms had fruited and were ready to harvest. I picked them and gave the mycelia–like the roots of mushrooms–a deep sniff. They smelled wonderful. I threw them into the compact desiccant dehumidifier.

They were ready by the end of the day. I collected the small amount of mycelia left behind–mushrooms are about 80% water–and brought them up to the kitchen. I pulled out the powdered sugar and water and got to work. I ground up the mycelia into a powder and threw it and water into a food processor for a few quick turns until I got a paste. My phone rang.

"Billie, do you have time now to tell me aaaaall about your night with Marti?" I did. I put the speaker on and kept working. I transferred the mycelia paste to a saucepan and placed it over low heat. The bioengineering job they did on this stuff was remarkable.

"When I got there, she was in her jacket and jeans, of course. I put her leather jacket on. Do you know how heavy that is? Plus, honestly, it smelled like sex."

I added powdered sugar to the saucepan and stirred continuously until it was fully dissolved. I told her about the rabbit vibrator, the boots and the underwear. More or less.

"What's with the underwear? You've done something like that before, if I recall."

The glaze is smooth and glossy as I give it a few last stirs. I stick the tip of my finger in and taste. Delicious, but it needed a pinch of salt. I removed it from the heat and cut thick slices of my day-after day-old breads, putting them on a baking sheet along with the pastries. "When I saw what she did the first time with my panties, it just blew my mind."

"Blew your vag, you mean."

"That too! I guess I just wanted to see if she'd do it again."

"And she did."

"With gusto."

"Did you give this woman a weird fetish for undies?"

I used a spoon to drizzle the mycelia glaze over the food on the sheet. It dripped into the nooks and crannies, pooling and sliding down the sides. "I think maybe I did." I tapped a small puddle on the sheet and a small drop stuck to my finger. I raised it to my mouth, and it was shockingly sweet. The glaze itself was fine. I'd already tasted it. I'd been thinking of Marti when I put my finger in my mouth. She's a lot muskier and a little saltier. "I have to go. Put these things out for folks."

A single pastry with the bio-engineered mycelia glaze would give someone about 40% of their daily nutrients and an extra 250 calories or so. It wasn't much, but it wasn't nothing.

I put the remaining glaze in an airtight container and threw it into the fridge. There was enough for about a week's leftovers. I wrapped each piece and put them out on the table before heading home. I realized Marti liked toast, and if I gave her a loaf of sliced, glazed bread, it would help.

Again. It wasn't much, but it wasn't nothing.

I opened the door of my apartment and stepped in, a piece of paper crunching underfoot. I stomped on it again a few more times. There was only one reason I would receive a piece of mail at this time of year: it was high school reunion time. I picked up the paper, crunched it into a ball, and stormed upstairs.

Chapter 26

I woke up surprisingly early on Saturday morning. I knew I would not be able to get back to sleep. It was almost 3 am, and I decided a shower and an early start at work were best. I didn't get as far as the bakery, despite the entrance being just feet from my door. When I walked down the stairs to the entrance of my apartment, I saw someone lying in front of the door. I managed to open the door with a lot of effort. He wasn't roused when I pushed the door against him and yelled for him to wake up.

I recognized him as a local addict who was always very thankful but very shy about the food I leave outside the bakery. He said his name was Lacrosse, but I didn't know if that was a first or last name. He was an old-looking man, though I doubt he was 40 yet. His teeth were mostly gone, from drugs and from fighting. He hid it under a big salt and pepper beard. I knocked on the glass to wake him up, but it didn't work. When I saw the pool of vomit, I called emergency services.

While on the phone, I ran upstairs and grabbed my naloxone kit. Naloxone is an opioid antagonist, and I was hoping a couple of auto injections would help keep him alive until help arrived, though I could not be sure what drug he was on. It might help, and it wouldn't hurt. I had been able to reach my arm out the door and get him in the shoulder. I used all three auto injectors by the time an ambulance arrived. When they took him away, he was alive, and they were working on him. But he never came back.

I started the ovens and prepped for baking. Despite Lacrosse, I was still earlier than normal. I went online to order more naloxone. I saw a message from Marti. I was surprised she'd written. She said she was heading to rehab and would be out of touch for a week. I hadn't mentioned it to her; I was glad she was trying again on her own. But I didn't hold out much hope for her staying clean. Sometimes it's best not to get your hopes up. I messaged her back, suggesting we go out for dinner when she gets back.

I wondered how many of her women contacted her, and how many had with an offer of dinner after she got out. I wondered how many women she had at this point. I knew of Faith and Eva by name, but none of the others. She never talked about them unless I asked. When I had asked her who took the photograph of her standing mostly naked in the rain, she dodged answering.

"Was it your secretary?"

"Nope. I'm not fucking my secretary."

"So it was sometime you were sleeping with?"

"We didn't sleep at all. We fucked."

"Well, who was it?"

"Why do you care? It's no concern of yours."

"But I'm curious."

"She'd probably join us one night, if you're that curious."

I was curious, but not that curious. Whoever she was, she was a good photographer. She had a good eye. She made me wonder about Marti's other women. She made me realize they were real people with real lives and real jobs and talents and needs and desires. It also made me wonder about a threesome.

The one I accidentally walked into seemed quite sedate. Eva was using a sex toy, while Marti and Faith made out. There was no "three" in the threesome that I saw. Not unless you include me when I kissed Marti. Just thinking about it again excited me. I was so lost in the thoughts of what could go on during one of these, I didn't see Grace arrive. She startled me with a greeting, and we got right to work, opening the bakery for our morning rush.

"Would you ever have a threesome?" I was sitting in the office, having my morning coffee and chat with Sandy. Grace and Jean were in the front, taking care of business.

"At this point, I'd be happy with a twosome. Kevin seems to be getting worse instead of better."

"So you wouldn't?"

There was a long pause. "I don't think so."

"What about if it was with Marti? You still have her photo, don't you?"

"I deleted it a little while ago. And no, not even with her. From everything I've heard from you, she's just too out there for me. You're getting quite the sex education, though. Does she sleep with men? Can I send Kevin her way? He could use some help."

"I don't think so. I've never asked. I still don't know what her 'everything' is. Oh, did I tell you? I got an invitation to Burnham High's thirtieth reunion."

"Oh God, you aren't going, are you?"

"No way." High school was horrible. I was taunted for being short, fat, queer, and ugly. I was called four-eyes because I had glasses, which is a stupid but long-standing insult. But wearing glasses meant your family was too poor for eye surgery, so more insults were heaped on. I was unathletic, and a bookworm. I graduated at age 17, went to university and never looked back.

"You know what I think is weird? There's this whole group of people who only know the past you. They know this kid they used to pick on, not the adult you've become. You're a very different person."

"I don't think about any of that unless it's thrown in my face, like this reunion invite."

"You need revenge," Sandy said. I'm absolutely someone who carries a grudge and seeks revenge. I sicced Marti on whoever was messing with my old pastries. "You need the ultimate revenge. Let them see how amazing your life is now."

"Sandy. My life is great, but it's not amazing. You can't beat these assholes, pardon my language. Someone will always have a better life than me. I'm okay with that. No revenge required."

"Okay Ghandi, take the high road. If I could get revenge on my school bullies, I would. If you go, wear a killer dress at least. Rent a limo. Treat yourself."

"I won't be going."

Three days later, Marti popped into the bakery. She stayed at rehab for one day, then left on day two. She told me every year for her birthday, she would go to rehab one day ahead of the date, and try to break her addiction. And every year, she failed, and spent her birthday "fucking hard and flying high." She didn't invite me because of the drug use, and I appreciated that. "I am sick of the psychobabble of well-meaning counselors who don't see just how full of shit they are. When Carl started on about a higher power, I just fucked off. This higher power is responsible for too much damage in the world. They can't see how they're part of the problem. Such fucking hypocrites." This was a side of her I'd never seen, and I did not like it. I changed the subject.

"I have a crazy idea."

"I love crazy ideas." She lit a cigarette and blew smoke out of her nose. As it dissipated, the old Marti returned.

"My high school reunion is coming up this weekend."

"Uh-huh."

"And I can bring a Plus One."

"Uh-huh."

"And I was thinking…" That was a lie. I hadn't thought about it at all. "Would you like to help me get revenge on my high school bullies?" She rolled her cigarette in her fingers and smiled before asking me who I wanted her to shoot. I gave her a smack on the arm and admonished her, and she pretended it hurt. I winged my revenge plan. I wanted Marti to show up looking gorgeous and seductive and make everyone jealous that I had a hot girlfriend. It had worked well at the art gallery, and I wasn't even trying there.

"No shooting?"

"No shooting."

"Not even a little bit?"

"Not even a little bit. I just want to show you off. I want everyone to think, 'Billie must be so hot to get a chick like that.'"

"You know it could backfire, right? I'm not the most reliable person." It was true. She was very unreliable. I had to make it worth her while to be reliable for just one night. My fingers trembled as I reached for her hand. She took my hand and it with the other, raised it to her lips and kissed my hand.

"What can I give you to inspire you? Wait! What can I give you that's legal, to inspire you?" I saw a flicker of an idea cross her face, but she just shrugged. I lowered my voice and said, "What about sex?"

"What about it?"

I offered her sex to come to my reunion, and she smiled but shook her head. "I am all for sex. Almost any sex. Pity sex, makeup sex, breakup sex. Are you breaking up with me?"

"No, no. Think of it as...reward sex. A reward for helping me get revenge."

She laughed at the suggestion. "But I'm already getting sex from you. It can't be a reward unless you're going to withhold sex. And you wouldn't want to do that. That's weaponizing sex, and that's not okay."

"C'mon Marti, work with me here. What can I give you that will inspire you to be part of my plan? Raspberry danishes for life? I'll clean your apartment and do your laundry for a month. Give you a month's worth of dinners." She gave me a bemused look. "Okay, look. I have to go back to work. Call me tonight with whatever idea you come up with."

She did not contact me that night. Nor the next. The reunion is tomorrow night, and I need an answer. Thanks to chatting with Sandy, I am now obsessed with the idea that Marti would be my high school bully revenge. I upped the ante. I sent her a message: "It's tomorrow night. I need you. I will reward you."

She messaged me an hour later. "Don't need a maid."

"Need bussy?"

She messaged me immediately: "Yours? Sold! See you there. Send info."

I stared at her response. I offered her pussy, and she responded with, "Sold!" I hoped she didn't think I was trying to buy her. Actually, I was trying to buy her. I had also expected her to pick me up, but her plan was to see me there. It would have to do.

I messaged her a few more times to confirm, but I heard nothing back. I gave Marti all the details: Burnham Secondary High School 30th reunion, Nolman-Cristi Hotel, 8pm, Saturday the 23rd. Still nothing. She'd bailed on me.

I was a nervous wreck, but Sandy built me up. "You can pull this off without her. Bring the photo of her in the rain, all your other pictures, so when they ask, you can show off." The rain photo was the only one I had that was even vaguely shareable. If I showed that, no one would believe me. I decided not to go.

Chapter 27

It was weird watching the clock on Saturday night. Seven o'clock came and went and I didn't turn into a rotting pumpkin. But something in me still fired up about showing up and showing off. At 8:00pm I called a taxi and grabbed the easiest nice thing I could find: my raspberry lingerie, a pale rose Ultrasuede pant suit, a simple white blouse, black kitten heels. I had no time for makeup, so planned to do the basics to my face on the way. Unfortunately, I had the driver from hell. He accelerated quickly, then slammed on the brakes when he caught up to the car in front. I spent the ride flinging back and forth, completely unable to do even lipstick.

It started to rain. Of course. I paid the driver and scrambled into the hotel. It was beautiful. I put on my lipstick, checked in at the registration table, and headed to the large room.

The grand doors of the ballroom swung open, revealing a scene of elegance, as if 2022 had anything unique to remember. At least the crappy blue medical masks didn't

make it in as a decoration. It was obvious that a professional planner had been hired to transform the interior of the
large meeting room into a stunning display of sophistica-
tion. The room shimmered with the soft glow of electric
candlelight and the gentle twinkle of fairy lights, casting an
enchanting ambiance over the gathering.

The ballroom had a tasteful décor and elegant drapes
in the school's colors, navy blue and gold, cascaded from
the ceiling, framing the expansive windows and adding
a touch of regal grandeur to the space. The walls were
adorned with framed photographs capturing moments
from past reunions. Photos of assholes hanging out with
assholes.

At the end of the room stood a magnificent stage, fes-
tooned with flowing floral arrangements and a backdrop
featuring the school's emblem. A live band played soft jazz
melodies. I don't think I've met anyone who likes soft jazz,
but it feels correct. The stage was flanked by towering pil-
lars adorned with twinkling lights, adding to the ethereal
atmosphere of the evening.

The seating area was arranged in circular tables draped
with crisp white linens, each adorned with elegant cen-
terpieces of fresh flowers and flickering candles. Gilded
chairs with plush cushions provided comfortable seating
for guests. The tables were meticulously set with sparkling
glassware and polished silverware. There was no formal

dinner planned, but I suppose some people eat finger food with a knife and fork.

Throughout the room, guests mingled and exchanged warm embraces, their faces alight with excitement and anticipation. Dressed in casual yet elegant attire, the attendees showcased a spectrum of styles, from sleek cocktail dresses and tailored suits to chic blazers and designer jeans. I scanned the room for Marti's distinctive leather jacket, but couldn't see it. I could do this without her. Why are so many people here so tall? It's hard to see past most of them, anyway.

Waiters circulated through the room, offering trays of tantalizing finger foods and drinks to guests. Miniature sliders topped with gourmet cheese, delicate canapés adorned with smoked salmon, and savory skewers of marinated chicken tantalized the taste buds, while trays of champagne, wine, and signature cocktails kept spirits high throughout the evening. The attentive staff ensured that no guest's glass remained empty and that every craving was satisfied. I grabbed some smoked salmon and a champagne. I casually chatted with a few of the high school outcasts who were still outcasts. How do you catch up on 30 years? None of us knew, so we caught up on only the last five. Mine was boring, without any mention of Marti. I owned a bakery; I didn't win the baking contest; I went to Paris. Yes, that Paris. No, I wasn't married, nor do I have children. Yes, I'm still queer. Yes, I do have a girlfriend, but it's casual. Sure, here's a photo.

That was a mistake. Laura Calderon had been listening, and she peaked over my shoulder. "No way Bill-Bill! Did you say that's your girlfriend? Wow, you are really punching above your weight."

"I prefer Billie."

"Hey girls! Come on over! Check out Bill-Bill's girlfriend." She made air quotes with her fingers when she said 'girlfriend'. The pack of hyenas came over, laughing and barking. I couldn't move, stuck in the cement of my teenage angst. I was 16 all over again.

"Girls, check out Bill-Bill's hot girlfriend," Laura said as she snatched my phone away. The other outcasts slunk off as the pack surrounded me. I began to sweat when the passive aggressive jabs started.

"Your girlfriend should sell her photos online. You know, to losers who need to pretend they have girlfriends. Too bad she isn't here tonight. She's real, isn't she?"

"You have your own bakery? How cute. That must be very fulfilling."

"I love how you don't care how you dress. It must save so much time in the morning."

"An Ultrasuede pant suit is so cool these days."

"I wish I could get away with just lipstick."

"So you finally got the eye surgery and ditched the glasses? Good for you."

I was feeling sick to my stomach. They had never left high school and here they were, dragging me right back into it. I couldn't think of what to say. I felt like that helpless teenager from 30 years ago. And then Laura got a strange look on her face. Like she was seeing a ghost.

I felt arms wrap around my waist, and I melted. Marti came in close behind, pressing against me. She kissed my cheek and murmured, "Hey honey, sorry I'm late." She let go of me and stepped into the circle of hyenas. A lion to protect me.

Marti took my breath away. She'd been to a stylist. Her hair was perfectly, sexily, wild. She had eyeliner and a subtle, glistening lipstick. She was wearing a crisp black silk suit with shiny black shoes. She wore a tight vest with the suit, and nothing more. No shirt, no bra. I wondered if she had underwear on. Her skin looked flawless. A gold necklace with a teardrop pendant hung down, drawing the looker's eye to her breasts.

She turned and kissed me. She stayed locked to me as her tongue probed me. When she finally released my lips, she gave me a big smile. I tasted whiskey and cigarettes on her. She'd been drinking. "You look..."

"Fuckable," she said.

"Very fuckable," I agreed, quickly glancing at the pack to see if they were scandalized. Laura certainly was. "Oh, my phone, please."

"I know this stylist, Eva…You met her at my place. She did hair and makeup for me for tonight. I, uh, paid her before I got the makeover, so it wouldn't be messy." She winked, gauging my response. She hasn't gone too far yet.

"Well, thank goodness for that," I said as I punched her lightly in the shoulder. People were looking at us, me, but it was with envy instead of the usual contempt. It made me feel good.

"I thought you'd wear a dress tonight. Can I just…" and she undid a button on my shirt. "Ah, there's the cleavage I love. And the raspberry bra! My favorite."

Laura introduced herself and the other hyenas. Then she introduced herself. "Martina Starova. Call me Marti."

"And you're with our little Bill-Bill? Wow! How did you two meet?"

Marti snagged two champagnes from a passing waiter, slamming one down so quickly she gave the empty glass back to the same waiter before he had time to pass. "Oh fuck, that's a story. I used to work homicide here in Falls City. April 26, 2049. We get to the scene of a double homicide, didn't even get to the door when this rookie cop comes over and says this crazy woman keeps asking about Heather, and screaming and crying. Well, our victims are John and Alice. I go over and ask who Heather is. She's the couple's 5-year-old daughter. Fuck! All hands on deck to find the girl! We hear from a neighbor they saw a man and girl run away just after they heard the shots. This guy has killed the girl's parents and kidnapped her. I run into the house and there are dozens of photos on the wall. I grab a bunch and hand them out. This is the girl we are looking for. It was…maybe 15 minutes since the emergency call came in." Marti has been loud and animated. Other people have joined the circle. She becomes more animated.

"This is Falls City. He could be anywhere by now! Everyone scattered, looking for the girl. I'm running up the street, showing everyone the girl's photo. Have you seen her? Have you seen her? Then I spot this old junkie under an awning. It's pissing rain. I have a river running down my face. I show the guy the photo. He points to a coffee shop across the street. I run toward the shop and I see them in the window. The bastard runs before I get there. I stick my head in and tell them to watch the girl, and I am gone. I am after this fucker, running through traffic, running down people, trying to catch up. He turns the corner. I'm closing in on him. I turn the corner. He's gone! I can't find him. It's pouring rain, I can't see shit. But then this glimmer of light catches my eye. It's the glass door of Billie's bakery shutting. I run over and see him, and run in. BAM! I tackle him. We slam into the plate window. It cracks, but then we're on the floor, hitting and kicking each other. He's putting up one hell of a fight, threw me into the display case and tries to run. No!"

She is in her full element now, wildly acting out the scene. The crowd has grown. Even the outcasts are back.

"So I make one last tackle, and I get him, but we hit the window. This time, we went through and in a shower of glass, we roll into the street. Right in front of a cruiser. My colleagues have finally caught up! Fuck. They arrest him and take him away. The little girl is okay. As okay as she can be. And I'm bleeding like crazy. He got me in the head a few times, and I had just gone through this big plate window. So I'm not thinking straight. I go back into the bakery. The rain is pouring in, there's broken glass and furniture everywhere. I walk up to Billie. Oh, beautiful Billie. I ask if she had any raspberry danishes, and she's just like...staring at me. She's like, pointing to the smashed display case, and she's like, 'Uh, no.' Real cool like that. But I'm still a bit loopy, so I just go over and grab a danish. One that wasn't too bad, and I bite it and shout, grabbing my mouth. She freaks out. I've just caused a hundred thousand in damages, and she's freaked out because she thinks I've hurt my mouth! Oh, the look on your face, baby. I just laughed and said I was joking, no damage done. She's like...what are you? She had no idea. But I fixed it. Didn't I honey? Fix it?"

"By the next day, everything had been repaired or replaced. I've never seen anything like it," I said. She was wild and beautiful, telling her story.

"That's unbelievable, almost like it's completely made up."

"Laura! Bill-Bill! Look! I found news articles on it with pictures. Here's Martina talking to the press and Bill-Bill, that's you in the background looking out through the window! You look so mad!" I was shocked. I had no idea there were photos.

"Well, double homicide is big news in Falls City. You might be able to find video too." Her words made everyone open their phones and start searching. No one was paying attention to us anymore, and Marti pulled me away from the hyenas. She kissed and nibbled my ear, whispering her plan to me: to cause unease at the reunion. Nothing major, nothing that can't be resolved, but enough to spoil the evening for some people, like Laura. I called her diabolical and gave her a big kiss. "They're trying to hang on to the time they peaked in life. Fucking high school. Pathetic. You okay?" I was better than okay.

I watched in awe through the evening as Marti "fucked with people."

We were standing at the bar, as Marti wanted a whiskey, when Genny walked up. "I hear you are a former police officer, so maybe you can settle a disagreement my husband and I are having. There is a local kid who is spray painting graffiti all over the place. Can I arrest him?"

"Are you a cop?"

"No."

"Then no, you can't arrest him."

"I feel like I can. There's the Citizens Arrest thing I read that said that I, as a citizen, can arrest people."

"That's true. And since you feel you can, sure, arrest the kid. Make sure you have the kid in handcuffs before you call the cops."

After Genny smirked and walked away, I confronted Marti. That was bad advice and Genny would be the one who got arrested. She laughed. "I know, but she'll probably get just a warning or a fine."

I was sitting at a table, and Marti, leaning against the back of the chair, was chatting with some men. I wasn't paying attention until I heard the words 'reward sex.'

"Reward sex is good. I do reward sex," Marti said.

"Every time I mow the lawn, I get to mow her." All the men laughed, but I didn't hear Marti laughing.

"But you get it other times too, right?"

"Sure, sure."

"Because getting sex after she withholds sex isn't a reward."

"What? Yes, it is."

"No way. Withholding sex until you do what she wants is transactional sex. It's a payment for doing something they want. Guys too. If you're like that, it's bullshit."

"Alright, what kind of reward sex do you get?" I turned around to stop the conversation, but Marti responded before I could say anything.

"Transactional sex is, do this thing and I'll fuck you. Regular sex is whatever your regular sex is. Reward sex is, you mow the lawn, and she rewards you by wearing a special outfit while you're fucking. It's the outfit that's the reward, not the sex. Or letting you do her in the back of your car, or whatever is special to you. That's what I mean by reward sex." I kept quiet because I wasn't sure I agreed with her, but I needed to think about it. Does it mean she'll want me to wear a particular dress? Or we'll do it in a car?

Marti headed off for another drink, but took so long, I became concerned. She had really been pushing the envelope tonight. If she drank much more, I was afraid she'd pull her gun out. I saw her with a group of people at the end of the bar, and she waved me over.

"Billie? Hey my sweet baby. Do you know Karen? Probably. Anyway, we were just talking about this beautiful necklace she's wearing." She reached out to trace the necklace with a finger and kept her eyes on Karen's. "Pearls. Beautiful. They really highlight your eyes." She was flirting with her. In front of me. I tapped her hand, hoping she would ease herself out of the conversation. What she did instead was wink at me. She leaned in to the necklace near Karen's face and pinched one of the pearls between her fingers. It reminded me of how she plays with my clit. She parted her lips, and I saw the desire growing in Karen's eyes. How Marti can inspire this level of lust in straight women is a puzzle to me. She hooked Sandy with just a photograph, and here she was, hooking Karen. "Oh! Fakes," Marti suddenly said as she snatched her hand back like the necklace was hot. "They're so realistic you almost had me fooled."

"They are real!"

"Oh, sorry Karen, they aren't. You can tell by the feel. They're smooth."

"My husband bought these for our anniversary. They're real." She clutched her pearl necklace and rolled them between her fingers. It was oddly satisfying to see her so doubtful.

"You can always take it for appraisal. I mean, I'm not an expert, but I know pearls aren't smooth. Listen, as a former cop, I'd recommend you take a few pieces in to a jeweler. Get them verified. Peace of mind, you know. Okay, well, it was nice meeting you, Karen. But I'd like to dance with Billie. C'mon baby, let's dance."

It was a slow dance. She pulled me closer, shoving my face into her cleavage, such as it is. She ran her hand down my hip and around my butt, gave me a squeeze, and kissed me. I watched throughout the night as she flirted with husbands in front of wives and wives in front of husbands. If they didn't flirt back, she dropped it and moved on. If there was the slightest interest, she'd let the person's partner know that she was not interested in a threesome and they should talk to their partner.

She was really good at creating discord. When someone's phone rang, she asked if people let their partners look through their phone. When someone complained about their nanny, she asked about parenting styles. When someone said they got a new job, she congratulated them and asked if they traveled. Who knew travel plans could create such dissent amongst almost strangers? The arguments were stupid and heated and I loved it.

The only people she was purposefully nice to, aside from me, were the Wilsons. She had worked the murder of their daughter, and she showed them kindness and compassion. They had nothing but love and admiration for her. The evening was intoxicating, and I was overwhelmed, but she took good care of me.

Chapter 28

Marti was witty and charming, despite all the drinking she was doing. She was really putting herself out there for me and I asked her why she was going so hard.

"Because I'm hard for you," she murmured in my ear while we were slow dancing again. "I can't wait for my not-a-reward." She squeezed my butt and kissed me. "We will need a whole day and night, though, to let me have full enjoyment." I was very confused, and let her know. "I mean, plan for time off work. I really want to take my time, you know? I know it's special for you."

The song ended, and she dragged me off the dance floor to a table. She sat in a chair and I straddled her lap, running my hands through her hair. I asked her why she changed her mind and decided to come to the reunion.

"I said yes."

"But then I didn't hear from you."

"I said yes. My mind didn't change. I said yes."

"Technically, you said 'sold'."

"I was buying what you were offering. How could I not agree? I promise I will blow your mind." She kissed me, and I was afraid.

"How are you going to blow my mind?" She ran her hands up the outside of my thighs and squeezed my butt again.

"We'll have to fuck for an hour or two to make sure you're turned on. Then I'll start with delicate kisses from the bottoms of your feet to the back of your leg, along your cheeks and between your crack. I'll kiss your beautiful, tight hole, my lips sending a shock through you." Her lips did send a shock through my body with those words. I was aroused and nervous.

"What are you talking about?"

"You offered your bussy, and I promise I'll treat you right. Respectfully."

"My pussy?" I whispered.

"Bussy. Butt. Your ass. Did you...did you not offer your ass? Let's be clear. I need to know 100% that you said I could have anal sex with you as a reward for turning it out tonight at this reunion."

Oh. Fuck. My mind turned madly, recalling my spelling mistake. I didn't know the word 'bussy' was real, and the word for anal sex. I never really understood her obsession with my ass, but she certainly lusted after it. I wanted and feared her lust. I was afraid her passion would consume me, take me down a road from which there was no return. I looked into her eyes, at her lips, and thought of her tongue in me. I couldn't help but clench my muscles.

"I felt that," she said.

"One hundred percent. You'll feel more."

"Be specific."

"Yes, Martina Starova, my ass is all yours." She kissed me and didn't stop until the band played another slow song. We were slow dancing. I had my head on her shoulder, my eyes closed. She smelled good, warm. I opened my eyes for a moment, saw that bitch, and jerked away from Marti. I was trembling, and she helped me to a table. I couldn't stop the fear in my eyes. Marti put her arms around me and held me, asking me if I wanted to go.

Charlene had caught my eye. I can still see cruelty in her face. I told Marti that Charlene spiked me a few times. She and her friends, some of whom were here, would jump me in the playground and drag me to a spike, the remnants of a sign pole. They would lift me up–I was much shorter than them–and they would thread the spike through my pants, underwear, and top, and then put my feet on the ground. I'd be trapped by this pole in my clothes and the only way to free myself was to undress, pull my clothes off the pole, and dress again. No one ever helped, not even teachers. I learned to wear skirts and button up tops. I could undo and redo my skirt and shirt quickly, and keep modestly covered. Then I'd slip my underwear off and since I had a skirt on, it wasn't scandalous. But it was humiliating, and I've not forgotten and not forgiven.

I whispered all of this to Marti and hadn't realized I was crying until she wiped a tear from my cheek. She put her face to mine and gave me a gentle kiss on the forehead. "Don't worry, I got you." I asked what she was going to do, and she said she wasn't sure. She promised no one would get hurt. "Oh God, here she comes." I felt like vomiting.

Charlene and her gaggle walked up to us and asked how much Marti had to drink this evening. "Enough to make you almost pretty."

"Think you're clever, do you?"

"Oh come on Carla, you can come up with better insults than that."

"My name is Charlene."

"You're thinking out loud, Charlie."

"Charlene. Charlene. Char-LEEN."

"You're boring me."

"To hell with you!"

"Speaking of which, where's the back exit? I need to get high. Back in a bit, babe."

With that, Marti got up and headed outside. Her words were like honey to a bee. Charlene pulled out her phone, very loudly said to her group "Stay here, I'm going to sneak up on her," and followed her out. Ten minutes later, Marti walked back in, but Charlene didn't follow. Her gang, who had left me at the table once the fun was over, was busy hounding a waiter for food. Marti told me she had lifted Charlene up and pushed her into a dumpster. "It's where garbage belongs."

We left before the event was over. I felt rejuvenated and thoroughly revenged. Marti was blitzed. She had me wait in the lobby while she tended to something, then we took one of the taxis waiting out front. I asked her where she'd gone: she went to make sure Charlene had made her way out of the dumpster. "People die in dumpsters. Couldn't have that."

We got to my apartment, and she followed me up after a few minutes. I knew she wanted a hit of Shadow, and she was very mellow when she came up. We undressed and sat in a big chair, wrapped under a duvet, watching the rain. The sky was a beautiful, thick black, glowing from the city lights.

"Gorgeous."

"It's a beautiful sky."

"I mean you." She lazily stroked my breasts, and I gave her a kiss. She was barely awake. "Let's go to bed." She looked around, confused. "I thought that's where we were," she laughed. I took the duvet and got into bed.

"I want to look at your pussy." She was slurring her words.

I parted my legs. "What do you see?"

"The universe." She kissed me, then crawled up beside me and fell asleep. I never imagined she could get so wasted that she opted for sleep over sex.

Chapter 29

I woke up alone, and it was a week before I heard from her. A message: "Tried and failed rehab. Dinner?" The message was simple but complex. Did the reunion drive her to rehab? Did Charlene press charges and her sentence was a stint in rehab? Was this an anniversary of some kind? The failure was not a surprise.

Dinners were an event that sometimes became sexual. Everything could become sexual with her. Was this dinner going to lead to the night? Did she even remember?

"Sounds delicious," I reply.

"Your pussy is delicious. Maybe that will be my dinner."

"I'm yours for the feasting."

"All night and all day buffet."

"I will take the day off. When and where?"

"Your place. Order food in. Tuesday 5pm?"

I was surprised by her suggestion, but agreed. I had three days to prepare myself. Sex with Marti was becoming more than a physical act. Maybe it always had been more. She was a magician, able to pull eroticism out of thin air. It might be a look, or maybe the way she inhaled a little deeper when she got close to you. You knew she was taking you in, a hungry animal smelling her prey. She must think about sex all the time. It's exhausting to walk around aroused all the time.

I learned what that was like over those three days. First, I had to clean my apartment. It was clean, but I wanted it cleaner. It wasn't just clean sheets and towels. I had to make the shower spotless in case we had sex there. And the vanity, in case we had sex there. I imagined sex with Marti on every single surface of my home. Never had I ever vacuumed my rug and gotten aroused at the thought of having sex on it, my face pressed into the fibers as she entered me from behind. As I wiped down the chairs, I thought of kneeling on the chair in the hotel while she ate me, and a shiver ran through me.

Once I was sure my home was clean enough, I focused on clothes. Would I need any? I should wear an amazing dress to greet her. I needed better lingerie and a new pair of shoes. Falls City is full of clothing stores, so I did not have to leave the city. I chose my lingerie first. Delicate Hearts is a lingerie boutique. There were no shrinking violets here. The staff woman asked three questions: Is the lingerie for sex? Who is this person to you? Will you see them again?

Yes. My girlfriend. Yes. The woman helped me pick a red lace bralette and panty set, but she steered me away from a garter and stockings.

"Is she a girly girl?"

"No."

"Then she will walk in, say 'Hey, pretty stockings. Take them off.' If you're really lucky, she'll take them off you. You'll wear them ten minutes, tops. Probably not worth the money, unless you really like them."

I wondered if Marti had a fetish for stockings, but I hadn't yet asked. I settled for the bralette and panties. They were expensive enough without all the extras. I didn't like the idea of ordering food in. It meant a stranger would be at my door. And no matter what, it would be outrageously expensive, and she would only eat the bread, anyway. So I opted to make a heart-shaped lavender bread and a sourdough French toast with a raspberry compote. I had enough time to allow 24 hours for cold-proofing the sourdough. That would result in a strengthened gluten formation, for improved structure so it would hold the compote well. With the sourdough prepped and in the refrigerator, I looked with a critical eye at my décor.

I wanted something warm, comfortable, and sexy. I refused to introduce any new scent: no perfume, no scented candles. No matter what, it would clash with the smell of baking bread. I shifted a few lamps so they were within reach of the bed and, on a whim, I put a large standing mirror against the wall opposite the bed. To check the placement, I sat in bed, leaning up against the headboard, and pictured Marti eating me while I watched her butt move around. It felt good, and I squeezed my legs together for a few seconds.

"All I can think about is sex. Is the place clean for sex? Am I going to look sexy for her? Will the bread smell sexy?"

"I'm sorry, what?" When I told Sandy I was baking, she clicked her tongue. "You must be serious about her if you're baking bread." So much of my relationship with Marti focused on baking. She destroyed my bakery, ate my danish, saved my 'free bread' program, rescued me from that guy and brought me to the safety of the bakery, kissed me in the bakery. She seems to only eat bread. So bread is perfect.

"It sounds to me like you're expecting a very special night."

"Well, I promised. I said that if she came to the reunion and looked gorgeous and…"

"And helped you get revenge, like I suggested."

"Tiny revenge, but it was so great. I offered her a reward for coming to the reunion."

"And she agreed."

"Not at first. But then I offered sex. I typed 'Need pussy?' and she's like, yes, absolutely. Except…I made a spelling error. I typed 'Need bussy?' Have you heard of that before?"

"Uh oh. No, what does it mean?"

"Butt sex."

Sandy howled when she heard. "You?"

"Yes, me. Can I ask you a deeply personal sex question? How risqué are you and Kevin?"

"He thinks taking his underwear off before he pumps and dumps is risqué," she laughed. "Why do you think I love talking to you so much about sex? It reminds me there's more to it than three minutes of foreplay and seven minutes of the actual deed. Billie, honey, baby, you are my reminder that sex is real."

"We never really talked this way while I was seeing Dierdre."

"You had no sex at all for the last seven years. Now you have this fricking model who lusts after you."

"She's not a mod–"

"She wants you in every way possible, for hours and hours. Hours, Billie."

"I'm not her only gir–"

"Stop it! I don't know why you are trying to play it down all the time. I mean, I get it. Dierdre treated you like a piece of shit, so you think you're a piece of shit."

"I don't–"

"Yes, you do. Repeat after me: I deserve a hot girlfriend."

"Sandy, I–"

"Stop. Repeat after me: I deserve a hot girlfriend. Say it."

"I deserve a hot girlfriend." I laughed and my cheeks burned from embarrassment. Why was I embarrassed?

"I deserve a woman who loves me."

She had me there. I know I deserve one. And I know Marti loves me, I think. "I deserve a woman who loves me."

"I deserve good butt sex. Say it."

I laughed for a solid five minutes after that. "What if I don't like it?"

"Has she ever touched your butt?"

"One time."

"And?"

"And I really liked it! She actually kissed my, like, butt, butt. Through my underwear. But I told her not to do that again."

"Oh baby, I love that, don't ever do it again. I don't deserve pleasure." Her sarcasm hurt me deeply, and I teared up. I couldn't say anything for fear of crying out loud. She knew why I was silent and apologized.

"Don't apologize. I do think that way sometimes." That I don't deserve it. That I haven't earned it. It can be hard to stop thinking long enough to start enjoying.

"Billie, what I am saying is, enjoy it while you have it. You have some hot young thing begging to make you feel good. Don't overthink it." Her advice was good, if painful. I'd already done so many pleasurable things with Marti I never thought I'd do: put her hand under my skirt in public, watch her have sex, kiss her while she's having that sex. We ended our conversation with Sandy asking me to tell her all about it, and me saying there was no way in hell I would.

Chapter 30

Marti is a master manipulator. It was on show when I opened the apartment door to her. She smiled, gave me a red rose and kissed me on the cheek. That single rose set her back at least $200. But it was excessively beautiful. As I breathed in the rose's luscious scent, its velvety crimson petals caressed my nose and lips. The fragrance was exquisite–a perfect blend of sweet floral notes mingling with earthy, verdant undertones. It evoked sensations of a wild garden after a summer rainstorm, when the dampened soil releases its musky perfume to mingle with the heady aromas of rain-kissed blossoms. The rose's stem was still slick with moisture, its dewy coolness refreshing against my fingertips. I could almost taste the tangy vibrancy of life pulsing within the freshly cut stem, its vitality not yet faded.

I pulled her in and shut the door, pressing myself against her, kissing her, holding her. "Hungry?" She ran her hand up my stomach to my breast and said, "Very." I pointed to the table and the freshly baked bread. I'd set out three different butters, a raspberry compote and some of my favorite cheeses.

"I'd like a different first course, and you're the most delicious looking thing here." She tossed her jacket onto the floor and it clunked: whiskey bottles. She pulled me toward the bed. The mirror stopped her short. She turned to me with a wolfish smile. "Let's play."

We stood at the end of the bed, facing the mirror, with me in front and her behind. She bit my ear and whispered, "Keep your eyes open, and watch." She wrapped her arms around me and toyed with my breasts, pinching my nipples gently until I could see and feel them rise up for attention. She looked into my eyes and slid her hand up my thigh and into the side slit of my dress. I watched the bulge of her hand make its way to my hair and felt a strong jolt as her fingers worked their way into my panties. Her fingers went to work.

Her eyes are a study in primal intensity. Gleaming with golden fire, they fixated unwaveringly on mine, radiating an erotic determination. With a sinewy movement of her powerful hand, her eyes narrowed into slits of pleasure.

I moaned and reached back to steady myself. She was ferocious, growling in my ear, making me even more excited. I closed my eyes, and she snarled, "Watch." I opened them again. I focused on her hand until I caught a glimpse of her eyes. Mirrored, I saw the untamed wilderness that held the secrets of her countless hunts. Her intense eyes were the silent communication between predator and prey, spoken in the language of passion. She squeezed and rubbed harder, bound by the rhythms of my ragged breaths. Her fingers continued their work on my flesh until I came, shivering in her arms as I soaked my panties. She moaned as I moaned and when I was done, she sucked on her fingers, humming.

She unzipped the dress and let it slip off me to the floor. "Let's eat," she said, making her way to the table. I didn't want to sit in wet underwear, so I changed them. "Can I have those?"

"They aren't your size."

"I'm not going to wear them," she laughed. I stuck them in her jacket pocket, slipped on a robe, and joined her. We ripped off bite-sized pieces of bread from the loaves and slathered on butters and cheeses and compote. We fed each other, kissed, laughed and murmured our dirty food attractions to each other.

"This butter is as creamy as you are."

"Dip your finger in and feed me."

"This is soft and sweet, like you."

"I'm getting sticky."

After eating, we both had food in places it didn't really belong. I had undone her shirt and put butter on her nipples and she returned the favor with raspberry. She put a smear of cream cheese on my neck and nibbled it off. No amount of licking will get rid of every trace, so we opted for quick, separate showers. "It's just too messy and time consuming to fuck in a small shower," she said. Marti took just a few minutes. I took longer as it gave me a chance to triple check that I was clean. I came out to find her with a cigarette in one hand and a bottle of whiskey in the other. Not much was gone, and she took a sip and put it down when she saw me. I thought it strange she had taken the time to clean up the food.

"Striptease for me," she said. I was wearing a white towel around my torso and one held my hair. I pulled off the one from my head first, tousled my hair a little more, and dropped the towel to the floor. As I took off the other towel, she held her hand out to take it, and laid it across the table.

"Bend over the table," she said. I did, and she ate my pussy. She rubbed her pelvis against my ass, tickling me with her pubic hair. When she was done, I stood up and devoured her breasts. She told me to lie face down on the bed and kissed my feet. She had said she would start this way, and I was scared and turned on at the same time.

She worked her way up my legs to my ass and asked if I was ready. "I want to kiss your asshole. Is that okay?" She didn't let me get away with a simple nod. "Say it out loud. All of it. Marti, I want you to kiss my asshole." When I did say it, I repeated it because it made my body jerk. She kissed and nibbled my cheeks and made me say it again.

"Kiss my asshole," I said, and she did. She kissed it with passion, humming the same way she did when she licked her fingers. The vibration felt amazing. She kissed over and over. I was about to erupt when she said, "I need to use my tongue. Can I use my tongue? I want to taste you, to go inside you with my tongue." I begged her to do it, and she did. I let out a scream before I was able to muffle myself with a pillow. When she went inside, I involuntarily clenched, making her moan. A wave of pleasure spread through me as I orgasmed. It was a mix-up of glorious contractions and pulses. When I was done, she covered me up, grabbed another shot of whiskey, and crawled under the covers.

When Marti says she wants to fuck all day, she is not joking. Day and night for hours. Twenty hours. We ate, fucked and slept. Well, I slept. She drank and smoked. We fucked on the bed, the table, the chair, the floor. Standing, sitting, kneeling, bending. Lying face up, lying face down. We said "Deeper!" and "Harder!" and "I love you!" What I was not expecting to hear was, "I need a hit."

"You...you want me to hit you?"

"No, I mean, a hit of Shadow. I know you don't like me getting high around you. So I guess I should get going."

She was right. I did not like it when she got high around me. I had foolishly thought the booze would be enough. That I would be enough. I was stunned. "You're going?"

She got dressed. "You don't want me getting high in front of you. Plus, I'm running low. I have to go out and buy a couple of inhalers. I hate running out. It makes my head hurt." That made my heart hurt. I watched as she tied up her boots and slouched on her leather jacket. She did not hide her need. I was just stupid enough to forget about it. My heart sank as she kissed me and walked out. I knew her addiction wasn't about me. Like any bomb going off, it wasn't personal, it only felt that way.

I spent the first few minutes expecting tears, but they didn't come. I forgave myself for making such an easy mistake, of forgetting she was an addict. I curled up and slept well.

Chapter 31

I didn't see Marti for another two weeks, and I didn't ask. I had my own problems going on. There was a break-in at the bakery.

Strike that.

An elderly African American man died during an arrest a little way down the street. He crossed the street against a red light, was arrested by four police officers, and died of a broken neck. The neighborhood erupted. Angry people took to the streets to protest, and the criminal element took advantage of the chaos. Someone drove a stolen car into the bakery, right through the glass window Marti had once sailed through. They stole food, broke windows and display cases, and threw supplies everywhere.

I cowered in my bathroom from the moment the car smashed into the building. I certainly couldn't go any-where.

I listened from my home above the bakery. Three minutes, and they were gone, leaving more than a million dollars in damages. Three minutes, and they destroyed my business and my home. My future. There was no point in calling the police. They were fighting in the streets already.

First, I called my insurance company. They said they deemed that the bakery was damaged by "people involved in an insurrection against lawful authority," and refused to discuss my claim further. Denied. It took them 15 minutes to deny my claim.

Next, I called the Victim Assistance Unit of the Falls City Police Department. Five minutes of being on hold, just to be told since it was not the police who did the damage, I was ineligible.

Less than an hour after the bakery was destroyed, and I knew I'd lost. It was a horrible sinking feeling. I hadn't felt like this since Li and Zhao said they were fleeing the country. But they had a plan—sell me the bakery. Now, I had no bakery to sell, no home to stay in. As soon as the police got people off the streets, I knew they would send in inspectors who would tell me the building was no longer safe. It was a damned car!

I called Marti. She'd help me once when the bakery was damaged, and I hoped she would help me again. I had to leave a message. "The riots, Marti, the bakery is gone. Help me." I collapsed into a heap on the floor. I screamed and cried and swore and shouted. I laid on the floor and kicked my feet and pounded my fists. I ran to the bathroom and threw up in the toilet.

When I woke up, I was on the bathroom floor. It took me a moment to get my bearings, remember why I was on the floor, figure out what the noise was. It was Marti calling me. When I answered, my tears started all over again. I wasn't sure I could survive this, but I thought certainly Marti could help me.

"Can you help? Call whoever you called before?"

"No, that was a cop thing. The Victim Assistance Unit won't help."

"I know. I tried. Is there anyone you know who can help?"

"I don't think so. I saw the news. The whole building is damaged. The damages…"

I begged and pleaded, but there was little she could do. "The only people I know with that kind of money are bad people, people who don't want a bakery. Look, I can't help you."

"I need your help. Just come over, please. I don't want to be alone right now."

"I can't. I'm with someone."

"I need you. I don't want to be alone."

"Look, I'm just not that person. I'm not going to hold you while you cry."

"You're an asshole."

"Yeah, yeah. I'll give you a call in a few days, okay?"

"No! No, it is not okay! How dare you brush me off like this?" I was furious. Absolutely livid. It was now clear that

I was not that important to her. "I am just one of your millions of girlfriends, aren't I? Nothing special, just one more pussy." I shouted and cursed at her every time she spoke until I'd had enough of her.

"Your bakery is not my prob–"

I hung up, my entire body trembling with rage. My phone rang, and I threw it against the wall. I felt cheated out of my life. I felt used.

My phone kept ringing, so I turned it off. I didn't know how long it took for someone to start pounding on my apartment door, calling my name. I headed downstairs to see. It was Sandy and Kevin. When I unlocked the door, they both rushed in and hugged me. Sandy led me upstairs to the kitchen table while Kevin secured the door and checked my windows. They had seen the news, seen the bakery. It was a top news story. They'd come rushing over, parking a mile away and sneaking past the police barriers to get to me. Sandy held me while I cried, while Kevin brought me water and rifled through the fridge to bring me a plate of leftovers. He might be bad in bed, but he was a damned good man.

Three days later, I settled into their spare bedroom. Kevin and his friends had moved everything from my apartment into a storage locker they rented for me. The city boarded up the gaping hole in the bakery wall and sent me a bill for $153,642.97. I had spoken to Jean and Grace, all of us crying when I fired them. It was heartbreaking. Everything was heartbreaking. I spent my time railing against rioters and cursing Marti's name. I know it is misguided. I knew it then, too. It wasn't Marti's fault. She had nothing to do with it. But she was an easy target.

So imagine my surprise when Marti left a message. "I have a buyer for your bakery. Meet us at Lia's Ranch on Aviator Road West, tomorrow at 5:00pm."

"Someone wants to buy the bakery?" Sandy was shocked. Kevin looked up from his phone. "Says here that's a brothel. Lia's Ranch is a brothel."

"Why would a brothel want a bakery?" No one had an answer, but I remembered Marti saying she only knew bad people with that kind of money. "Billie, take Kevin with you when you go. He'll keep you safe."

"I don't think that's necessary. Marti is a heartless demon, but she's always kept me safe."

Lia's Ranch was old school pretty, with floral wallpaper, silk draperies and leather seating. When I walked in, there were almost-dressed women sitting around, waiting for clientele. They looked at me with indifference and I at them with nonchalance. I went to the reception desk. A beautiful blonde sat in a bustier at the counter, a faded mirror behind her. Before I opened my mouth to speak, someone knocked from behind the mirror, and the receptionist said, "Please go in." She pressed a button and a door to the side buzzed and unlocked. I felt like I was in one of those old private eye movies where secret doors lead to clandestine meetings.

And it did. The mirror was a one-way window into the brothel corridor. There were security cameras outside every room, their feeds displayed on a bank of computer screens. A security guard monitored everything. Marti sat in an armchair, smoking. Behind the mahogany desk was Lia Fisher. She wore a pretty top and her hair was done up nicely. She looked like an accountant, not a brothel owner.

"My style is to get right to business," Lia said as I sat down across from her. "Marti told me about your shop and said you might be interested in selling."

"I'd rather find an investor."

"No one is going to invest that much money in a bakery. I sent an inspector to the property, had my lawyer look at the property title and taxes. My guy said it will cost at least $400,000 to bring the building back, meet safety codes, building codes, whatever."

This woman was organized, and way ahead of me on this. "I thought it would be more to repair. I thought–"

"I'll get it done for cheaper than you. I've got good connections in the construction industry, so I get discounts." I didn't much care for the side eye she gave Marti. "You have no mortgage, no liens. Taxes are high but manageable. The property values halved after the riots."

"I jus–"

"Let me finish. I'll buy the building from you for $600,000. Cash in your account. Marti tells me you care about your business, your customers. Me too. I'll run the bakery myself. I'll move into that apartment above the store. I'll hire your old staff if they still need jobs. I've got a lot to learn about baking."

It seemed strange to me that this woman wanted to start running a bakery. When I asked why, she said she is selling the brothel. I asked why and she said it was none of my business. And it wasn't. "So, $600,000?" To the side and slightly behind her, Marti very subtly shook her head. She was an asshole, but she always looked out for me. She held up one finger, then five fingers.

"One point five million for the property and all goods and chattels, immediate possession."

"Wow, that's a hell of a valuation. I'll go up to $700,000." Marti held up one finger, then four fingers. God, I loved the feel of those fingers.

"One point four million." I felt a sheen of sweat form on my brow and I prayed it wasn't obvious. Marti winked.

"Nothing personal, but that's crazy. I'm sticking with $700,000."

"Nothing personal, but $1.4 million." Marti flashed one plus five. "And if you try to go lower, I'll ask for $1.5 million again."

"Fuck, Marti, why didn't you warn me she's a hard ass?"

"Her ass is soft until she flexes her muscles, then it's hard as fuck."

"Shush, you. One five."

"One three. Final offer," Lia said, extending her hand. Marti flashed her eyebrows and a slight smile.

"Deal." We shook hands. Later that day, I contacted a real estate lawyer. The next day, the paperwork was signed. The building was hers and I had a future again. It was almost a goddamned fairy tale.

Chapter 32

I stayed with Sandy for another month while I organized my life. I bought a small deli in Cliffport, where the baking competition was held every year and where the sun shone. It took almost every penny I had, but I knew I could make it work. I'd be glad to get out of the rain. Marti reached out to ask how I was doing and if I wanted to fuck before I left for good. I told her I was fine, and of course, I wanted to fuck.

We met at her place, since I wasn't about to bring her to Sandy's home. I asked her to wear a white tank top and jeans. She asked me to wear my raspberry lingerie. I was in luck: it was pouring rain. I had a lingering fantasy with Marti ever since she sent that photograph. When I arrived, we kissed and groped until I asked her to go onto the fire escape.

"Stand in the rain, open your fly," I told her as she stood in the rain. Her nipples were rock hard as she stuck her hand into her pants. I crawled out with her, kissing her, pinching her nipples, pulling up her soaking wet top and stroking her breasts. She pulled me close with her free hand, and I kissed her hard. I could feel her fucking herself and got so excited, I pulled down her pants, kneeled before her, and lavished her pussy with everything I learned. She squirted on my face when she came, but it was quickly washed off in the rain. We laughed and as I leaned through the window to return to the apartment, she pulled my panties down and ate.

In the soft light of dawn, I watched Marti sleep, knowing that I hadn't needed to fear her darkness, but to embrace it as a part of her flawed and fiercely vibrant life. Despite her faults, she is the most beautiful animal I have ever known.

I miss her sometimes, in the early morning sun, when I'm having a coffee and staring out my window. I've moved on with my life, and I am certain she has moved on with hers.

Epilogue

I got a call from Sandy this morning with some news. It's been almost two years since I moved, but she thought I should know. Marti had suffered four gunshot wounds and was in the hospital. She was a bystander in a gunfight between Federal Agents and some drug kingpin. I was grateful she'd survived. I cared about her, but didn't–couldn't–reach out. The person I once loved, who once loved me, would forever be at the edge of her world, running into the abyss.